KEVIN BERRY

Shooting Messengers

A contemporary crime noir novel

First published by Quake City Publications 2020

This novel is entirely a work of fiction. The names, characters and incidents portrayed in it are the work of the author's imagination. Any resemblance to actual persons, living or dead, events or localities is entirely coincidental.

Cover design by Dawné Dominique, DusktilDawn Designs.

Quake City map by Ava Fairhall.

The story is written in UK English.

Second edition

ISBN: 978-0-473-51533-1

This book was professionally typeset on Reedsy.
Find out more at reedsy.com

Acknowledgement

I wish to express my thanks to Charlotte Kieft (who writes as Charlotte Jardin), Eileen Mueller, Lee Murray, A J Ponder, and Mark Johnson. These friends are all talented writers who encouraged and helped me immensely with this story. I hope some of my readers will take the time to look them up and read some of their work.

Ava Fairhall designed a beautiful, detailed map of Quake City, which is reproduced on the following two pages.

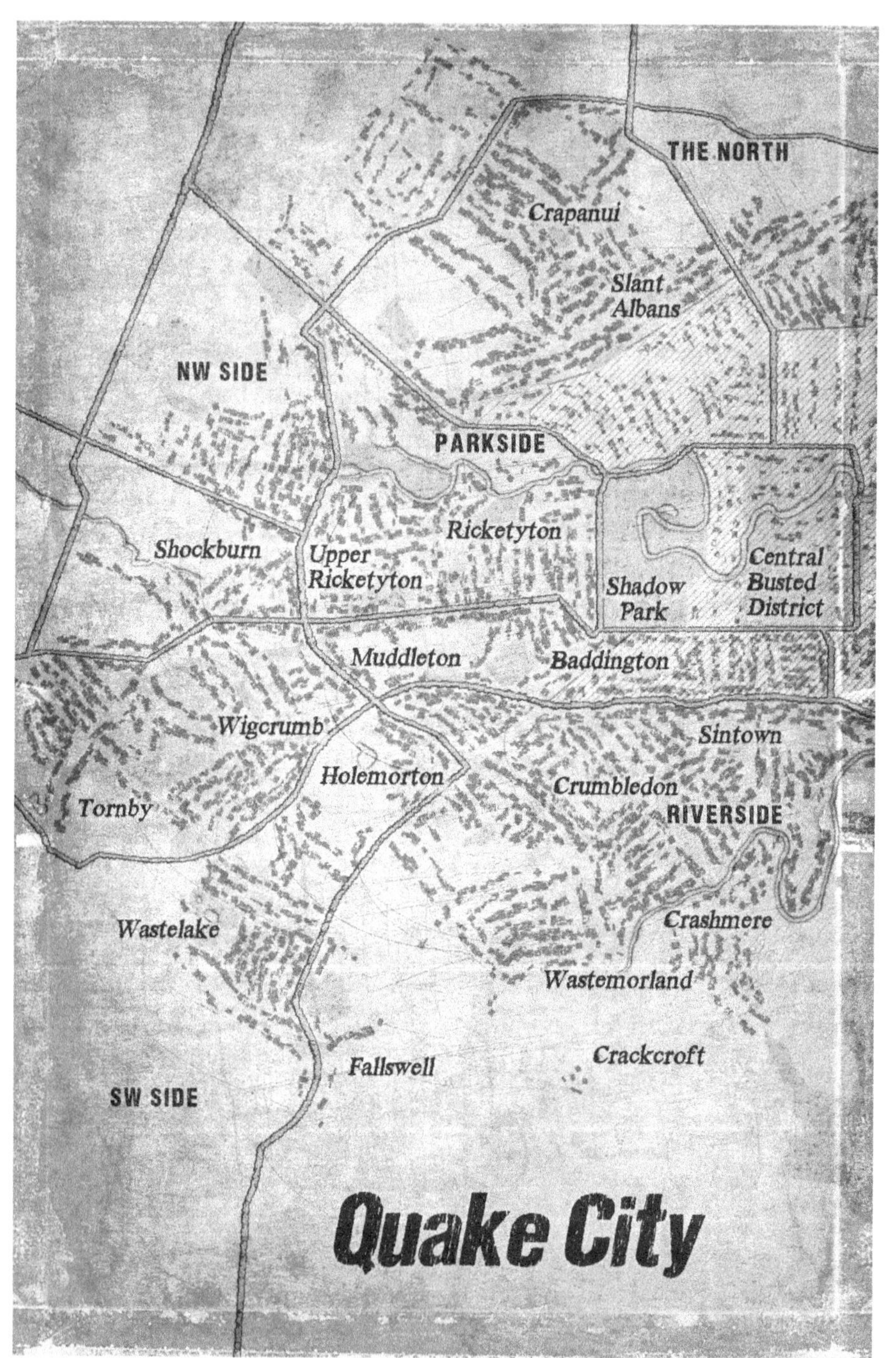

THE NORTH
Crapanui
Slant Albans
NW SIDE
PARKSIDE
Shockburn
Upper Ricketyton
Ricketyton
Shadow Park
Central Busted District
Muddleton
Baddington
Wigcrumb
Sintown
Holemorton
Crumbledon
RIVERSIDE
Tornby
Crashmere
Wastelake
Wastemorland
Crackcroft
Fallswell
SW SIDE
Quake City

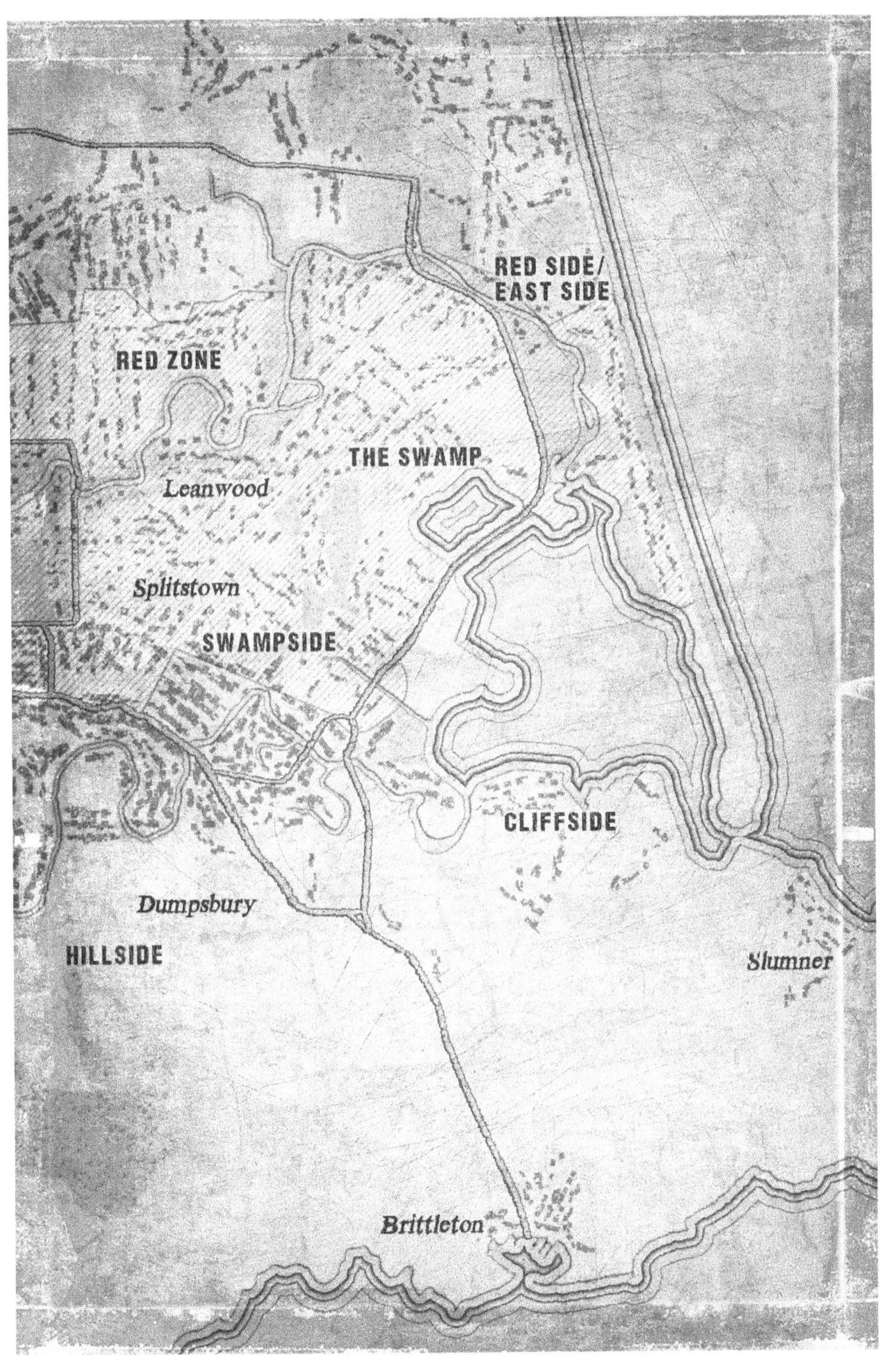

RED SIDE/ EAST SIDE
RED ZONE
THE SWAMP
Leanwood
Splitstown
SWAMPSIDE
CLIFFSIDE
Dumpsbury
HILLSIDE
Slumner
Brittleton

Chapter 1

Day 1, morning

CLIENTS HAVE ASKED ME to find a variety of things in my work as a private investigator, but no one's ever before asked me to find a story.

Deepa Banwait, investigative reporter, paced back and forth across my office, her voice quick and shrill, her shoes squeaking on the wooden floor whenever she turned. I sat back in my creaky chair at my rickety desk, listening and following her progress with my gaze. It was like watching a tennis match from a mid-court position. My cat, Torquemada, watched her too, from on top of a crammed bookcase.

She wanted something from me.

The thing was, I owed her a favour. A big one. She'd saved my life on a previous case and getting an interview out of me wasn't enough repayment for her. Deepa wanted more. She wanted me. Or, rather, she wanted my investigative skills.

Deepa collapsed in the high-backed chair opposite me, leaned her laptop bag against its leg, and clutched her hands together. "Will you help me, Danny?"

I regarded her with interest. Deepa was a petite woman in her early thirties of Indian descent, attractive, yet as slim and muscular as a marathon runner. Her purple puffer jacket, hanging on the back of the chair, rustled as she shifted in the seat. A faint scent of French perfume wafted across my desk.

I pulled myself together. "Let me get this straight. You want me to investigate a murder and see if there's some background story you can write up and get published in the *Richter Mail*."

Her eyes widened. "No, I want us to investigate it *together.* Take me with you. Show me how an investigator works."

"I work alone."

"We made such a brilliant team last time."

"We weren't a team. I did all the hard work. All you did was take photographs and pull me out of the sea."

She beamed, her teeth glinting in the light coming through the slatted blinds behind me. "That's why you need me. As back-up."

I frowned. "What are you going to do if we work together?"

"Take notes. Write up the investigation as it unfolds. Earn the money."

Ah. Money. Good. A man's cat has to eat, after all, and I had no other work at the moment. "All right. My fees are eighty dollars an hour plus expenses, with five hundred upfront—why are you shaking your head?"

"I can't do that. The newspaper won't pay me until after they publish the story—if there is one to write about. If we find something juicy, and I can sell a few articles about it, then I'll split my earnings with you down the middle."

So, there was no certainty of even being paid for this job. I leaned forward. My chair creaked, emphasising what I was about to say. "Why don't you investigate it yourself, Deepa? Why involve me?" What's her real motive here? Is she keeping something back? Does she want me to train her as an investigator? Or get close to me?

She bit her lip and stared at the floor for a few moments. "My usual work's drying up. I need something different, something big. But murder's… intimidating." She looked up and gazed at me with brown eyes as pleading as Torquemada's when his dinner's late. "I sense there's a hidden story behind this one. Please understand, I'm not asking you to solve the murder itself, only help me dig out the background stories behind the people involved."

I narrowed my eyes. "And then you'll write it up for the newspaper? You'll exploit the pain of the victim's relatives, depriving them of their privacy at a time of grief?"

She shook her head. Her jet-black hair, tied in a ponytail, swung in a strangely captivating way. "What I do is tell the whole truth. When someone's ready to talk, that's when I approach them. I write the tough stories, the ones other reporters can't find or don't want to put their name to. I get the genuine story out into the world, not just the facts of the matter. I humanise it."

That sounded respectable, rather than exploitation. I exhaled my held-in breath and stared straight at Deepa. "Are you sure you want to be a crime journalist? Why?"

"The editor said my piece about the drowned dockworker was awesome. He wants to see more crime writing from me." She tilted her head. "And it's more interesting than covering local events."

I nodded. Her goal made sense. "Okay. What murder are you talking about? When and where did it happen?" Crime in the run-down suburbs of Quake City was rampant.

Deepa glanced at her slim silver watch. It was elegant and suited her. "My police source called me twenty-five minutes ago and told me that someone shot a postal worker on his round. I wasn't far from your place here in Crumbledon, so I came straight away."

"You're serious about this, aren't you? But tell me one thing: what makes you so sure you'll find an exciting story? The police will already be investigating. Reporters will be all over it like ants over sugar—no offence—for tomorrow's paper. What makes you think there's more for us to find than they will?"

"My source says the police already suspect it's the work of a serial killer. There'll be a story behind that for sure."

"But there's only been one murder."

"Apparently, the police think that's just the start."

I sighed. "The investigating officer is Inspector O'Toole, isn't it?"

"Yep. How did you know?"

"He's obsessed with serial killers and has made it his mission in life to apprehend every single one, real or imagined. If he captures someone after a single murder, he pats himself on the back for preventing umpteen more that would have followed."

Deepa rapped her feet on the floor, impatient. "Even so, I want to look into it, and find the story I'm sure is there. We should get to the crime scene now, while the police are there." She stood, as if implying that was the end of the conversation, then stopped. "Hey, maybe you can come up with a psychological profile for the killer too."

I raised an eyebrow. "Profiling as well. Anything else?"

She shrugged. "I'll think about it. Are you coming?"

I concentrated on what was most important. "I'm still not sure if I'll get paid for this if I help you."

She smiled, and my resistance melted. "Look at it this way, Danny. Do you have anything better to do right now?"

Only talk to the cat and contemplate my ever-growing pile of unpaid bills.

Chapter 2

I DONNED MY BROWN FEDORA and navy-blue raincoat. It was important to look like a private investigator if I wanted potential clients to take me seriously. The long raincoat served that purpose as well as warding off the cold. Besides, it had many pockets that came in useful for all sorts of gadgets and equipment. And my home-made business cards. And, at times, a Glock 17 handgun that I'd appropriated from a criminal for my own use.

Deepa and I made our way to the crime scene in my peppy blue Suzuki Swift. Not the typical ride for a private investigator, but it was cheap to run and never broke down. Our journey to the nearby leafy suburb of Crashmere took ten minutes, delayed by the perpetual roadworks that had spread like cracks across a windscreen around Quake City following the earthquakes that had given the city its name.

Crashmere was an affluent area, and lucky. The quakes had spared the houses, apart from toppling their chimneys and crumbling a few walls. But the roads were wrecked, the asphalt cracked like crazy paving, and there was no sign they'd be fixed soon.

Patrol cars jammed the road half a block in either direction. I parked across a driveway behind one of them.

A yellow and black crime scene tape cordon was in place to prevent curious onlookers from moving closer. We approached a young female constable and showed our credentials: Deepa's press card and my private investigator's licence. On the late winter's morning, my breath clouded as I exhaled. Frost lingered on the shadowy parts of front lawns.

The officer held up a gloved hand. "Sorry, guys, they're still processing the scene. You'll have to stay out here like everyone else."

We backed away, out of earshot.

"What do we do now?" Deepa stood, arms akimbo, lips pursed.

"We watch and learn what we can." I took a pair of mini binoculars out of one of my raincoat pockets and peered through them. The image of a Scene Of Crime Officer, a SOCO, bending over the ground, searching for clues, burst into my vision.

"I've got a zoom app on my phone." Deepa whipped an expensive Samsung out of her bag. It was probably worth more than my car. Being an investigative reporter must pay damned well. Maybe I would earn something from this gig after all.

Forensic photographers prowled the area, recording the scene and the evidence with digital cameras.

"I can't hear what they're saying." Frustration crept into Deepa's voice.

"Me neither."

The coroner peeled back a plastic sheet covering the body and examined it. I zoomed in for a closer look at the gory sight.

The postman lay prone on the frosty grass, one arm bent beneath his body at an odd angle, the other arm outstretched towards the letterbox. But the blood-soaked letter clutched in his hand would never be delivered. The stain seeped into the grass. The postman's glassed-over gaze fixed upon the letter as if it were to blame. I grimaced at the gaping bloody hole in his back, my stomach clenching. My breath hastened. This killing had been brutal.

Poor guy. But at least death had been instant. Never again would I complain when the post was late, or when it comprised only the latest bills.

I glanced at Deepa to see how she was taking it. Had she seen a dead body before? Someone murdered? I didn't know.

Deepa's gripped her phone, her knuckles white. She stared at the scene, eyebrows furrowed, unable to divert her eyes. I reached out and lowered her arm so the phone's magnification wouldn't reveal so much.

"Do you ever get used to seeing this?" Her face was pale.

"Not really. You must distance yourself from it if you want to be a crime reporter."

I looked back at the scene. The postie's red electric delivery vehicle, no larger than a golf buggy, stood only two metres from the corpse, undamaged. Someone had switched it off. The killer had attacked the postman when he'd gotten out to deliver the letter.

But who would want to kill a postie? And why?

The coroner covered the body, providing the unfortunate man some dignity in death, his corpse no longer something for curious onlookers to stare at. Good. There could be neighbours peeping out, even children who shouldn't see that grisly sight.

Deepa pointed. "Hey, look. The SOCOs have found something on the road."

I refocused to where a SOCO was marking a circle about fifteen metres from the body. "Looks like shotgun cartridges. Two of them."

An enormous eye appeared in my view, startling me. I lowered my binoculars. The female constable I'd spoken to before confronted me, scowling.

"What do you think you're doing?" Her voice had icicles.

"My job."

"Put those binoculars away. This is a serious crime scene, not entertainment."

"There's no law against me viewing through binoculars, is there?" I noticed she hadn't complained about Deepa's phone, which was more circumspect.

The constable harrumphed and returned to the other side of the cordon.

"So, Danny, what's going through your mind right now? Where would you start investigating?" Deepa had the voice recorder activated. She thrust it at me. Her voice had a tremor and her fingers trembled, but she was trying to do her job.

"I thought you wanted the stories behind the murder, Deepa? The victim's background. The killer's motivation. That's what we're looking for, isn't it?"

"Yep, that's right, but at the moment, you're it. I'll write the story of how you go about investigating this case."

So, she wanted me to solve the murder after all. That wasn't our agreement, but my initial thoughts might help her write something. There was no harm in showing her how a private investigator worked—and if she sold the article, at least I could pay some of the bills and feed the cat.

I pointed down the road, where one constable poked around under a hedge and another used his baton to prod a rose bush.

"They're still looking for the murder weapon. Of course, the perp may have taken it with them."

"Perp?"

"Perpetrator."

"Right. I see. It's PI jargon."

I thrust my hands in my pockets to keep them out of the chilly air. "The killer is probably male. That's usually the case with shootings. Though we can't know for sure."

"Okay. Any more insights?"

"There were two shots. The shotgun cartridges are on the road, so the perp could have been standing there, or sitting in a car. I'd guess a car for a quick getaway. One shot hit the victim, and the other hit a tree behind the victim. See where a SOCO has marked a circle on a tree trunk over there?"

Deepa peered across the road through her phone camera. Her face was still pale, but at least she'd stopped trembling. "Yep, I see it."

"See how they line up? That tells us the killer was stationary when he or she fired. Was the postman killed by the first shot or the second? Unfortunately, we won't know unless a witness tells us later."

"Does it matter? He's still dead."

"It might. Let's say the first shot missed. Maybe the perp took the shot in haste, or maybe they're a poor shot. If the killer missed from that range, why? Weren't they trained to fire weapons? That would rule out people with military experience, suggesting the killer's a civilian."

"Ah, I get it. You're coming up with a profile. So, what if the first shot killed the postie, and the killer fired a second shot afterwards? Would that suggest someone who's trigger-happy? Has a nervous trigger finger?"

"Possibly. It's all theoretical at the moment. Look at the relative positions of the postal vehicle and where the shells were found, and that the postman was shot in the back. He never saw his killer."

"Is that important?"

"Yes. It doesn't match the profile of a professional hitman. They like to get close to the victim, identify them by sight, then execute. And they don't miss."

"I see." Deepa stuffed her free hand into her jacket. We could still see our breath clouding in the chilly air.

"Finally, I'm thinking: Was the murder pre-meditated or random? Was the postman a target for some reason, or just in the wrong place at the wrong time?"

"Could the police use traffic cameras to see where the car went?"

"No chance. The city council hasn't maintained the cameras since the big quakes. Hardly any of them work anymore, and there's probably none around here anyway, as it's a suburban street."

A gruff voice interrupted. "What are you doing here, Ashford? And who is this lovely woman with you? Girlfriend?"

She spun to face him. "No. I'm Deepa Banwait, an investigative reporter." Deepa snapped the last word.

That was firm. My only response had been to blush, but I regained my equilibrium and introduced them to each other.

Inspector O'Toole was in his fifties, with a ginger moustache and short beard and an eczema condition. He wore a neat sports blazer, despite the cold. Obviously, he hadn't yet worked out how useful long coats were.

"You haven't told me why you're here, Ashford." He ran his fingers over his beard.

"Professional interest, Inspector. As always."

"The murder only happened an hour ago. The body's still warm. We haven't even released the victim's name to the public. How did you know about it so quickly?"

"A contact of mine brought it to my attention, Inspector." I didn't see the need to explain that Deepa was the contact in question, though I caught her sharp glance in my direction.

Deepa thrust her voice recorder forward. "Inspector, do you believe this is the work of a serial killer?"

O'Toole puffed his chest out. "Undoubtedly. We have a seemingly motiveless murder carried out at random. The victim still had his wallet, so we're discounting robbery. This violent and arbitrary shooting is a classic sign of a serial killer. And I intend to catch him before he kills again. There'll be a press briefing at five p.m. You're welcome to attend, Ms Banwait." The inspector turned to go.

"I see what you mean about his serial killer obsession." Deepa gave a wry smile.

I nodded but didn't share her smile. A chill crept up my spine, despite my coat and fedora.

Chapter 3

Day 1, afternoon

WE SAT IN MY CAR, out of the cold, while the SOCOs worked the scene. Deepa typed on her laptop. I pulled my fedora low over my head and closed my eyes. Let my subconscious go to work.

Deepa's voice stirred me. "What should we do now? The crime scene is still off-limits."

I roused myself. What had seemed like moments had been half an hour. My stomach rumbled. "Lunch. We can't work on empty stomachs. There's a McDonald's near here."

We drove to the McDonald's and went inside to eat. Deepa ordered a salad and poked at it with a fork, eating almost nothing.

The hubbub of conversation gave us privacy to talk in our own space.

I munched on my gourmet creation, watching Deepa play with her food. "You don't like it here? Maybe we should have gone somewhere else." But I was the investigator here. She was only tagging along.

"I don't know how you can eat after seeing the body." She shoved her meal aside and tilted her head. "I've been thinking about how you talked me through the crime scene. That was smart analysis. Did you ever think about joining the police force?"

"Nah. Too many rules and too much paperwork."

"Okay, I get that. So, you became a private investigator instead. Was that because of what happened to your parents?"

Now it was me losing my appetite. I put my food down. "How do you know about that?"

Deepa shrugged and opened her laptop. "I did a little research on you. I wanted to find out what makes you tick."

"I see. And did you?"

"Not really. Only that you worked for a detective agency, then left and started up Quake City Investigations to work on your own."

I cleared my throat. "That's how I like it."

"So I gathered." Now she was typing fast. "And were the criminals responsible for your parents' murders identified?"

"I thought you said you didn't prey on people's grief." I looked down, my appetite gone now. Nausea and a sense of weakness spread through me.

"Sorry to pry." She glanced up, solemn, but kept typing.

"Sorry, my ass." It was bad enough having Deepa accompany me on working the case, but I hadn't expected her to grill me on my personal history.

"That's enough for now, then." She seemed oblivious to my annoyance. Maybe that's what happens with reporters after a while. They develop an attitude to get a story at any cost. My shoulders and neck tensed. What had I gotten myself into with this agreement?

I folded my arms. "Are you going to write about me? Why?"

She contemplated me. "My readers want to know the story behind the story. They'll want your expert preliminary assessment of the case. To make that sound credible, I need to explain a bit about who you are, how you know what you're talking about… that sort of thing. Okay?"

Deepa would lay aspects of my life bare on newsprint and digital pages to satisfy the curiosity of strangers. I fumed for a moment, then shrugged it aside. I hadn't said much. I might not like it, but it was basically free advertising, and might attract more clients. Perhaps that wasn't a bad thing.

"I need to get back to the crime scene." I pushed my half-eaten burger away.

"I'm coming with you. I'll finish writing this later." She closed her laptop.

We left with a couple of takeaway coffees and drove back to the murder scene. The police tape remained, but the SOCOs and photographers had gone. One constable stood guard, though he let us into the area when I showed my ID. The day had warmed a little, but it was still overcast.

"I want to question potential witnesses." I indicated the house next to the one by where the perp killed the unfortunate mailman. "The inspector and his sergeant went in there, and a police counsellor. The occupant probably called it in."

"That's astute."

"It's just observation, that's all. The difficulty is with getting the person to talk. They've already told the police whatever it is they know, and often they don't want to go through it all again. Especially if it's traumatic, like this."

"That's what I'm here for. Getting people to talk."

I shook my head. "The witness might not want to talk to a reporter. They might talk to me, though, as I'm an investigator. Like the police."

"And if the witness doesn't want to talk to either of us, what then?"

"Don't worry about that. I have a sure-fire investigative technique."

A chalk outline marked where the postman's body had lain. That wouldn't last long with the forecast rain. I shuddered as we skirted it.

The path next door led to an expansive house. A dark Mercedes squatted in the driveway like a self-satisfied cat about to purr. The curtains twitched, then stilled. I knocked and waited.

A lady in her fifties with long auburn hair answered. Her long red dress swished in the breeze. She eyed us with a raised eyebrow. "Can I help you?"

"I'm Danny Ashcroft, a private investigator, and this is Deepa Banwait, investigative reporter. We'd like to ask you about what happened earlier today."

"I've already told the police everything." She started to close the door.

I put my foot against it. "Please. Just a few minutes of your time. My client wants to see justice done. And we are working with the police." That was stretching the truth a little—or a lot—but I didn't care if O'Toole found out about it. I had something on him, and he knew it.

"All right. You'd better come in. My name is Monica Kennedy."

We settled in the living room, and Deepa took out her notebook. Warm air fanned me from the heat-pump above the sofa. It was a comfortable, fashionably furnished space.

I leaned forward. "Please tell us what you saw."

"Well, as I told the police, I didn't *see* anything. It was the sound that alerted me. Two loud bangs, it was. Oh, they gave me a fright. At first, I thought it was another earthquake, but then I realised it wasn't. It was more like a car backfiring."

"What made you call the police?"

"Once I was sure it wasn't another aftershock, I went to the window to look for the car. Teenagers have been racing down the street lately. By that time, I was *quite* sure that it had been a backfire—"

"Did you see a car?"

She shook her head with an exaggerated motion. "No, but I heard a car's engine revving as it drove away. Then I saw the postie's vehicle, and when I went out to check if I had a package—from online shopping, you know—I saw him lying there... covered in blood..." She sobbed and covered her mouth with her hand.

"Sorry, Mrs Kennedy... Monica... I didn't mean to upset you. That's all we need. You've been very helpful. Deepa, would you fetch a glass of water for Mrs Kennedy, please?"

Deepa did so and sat with her for a minute or two until she'd recovered her composure. Then we thanked her and left.

I turned to face Deepa with a smile. "What do you think?"

"Of your special investigative technique? Was that it, putting your foot in the door?"

"I meant, what do you think of what she told us?"

Deepa shook her head. "Not much help. Why didn't you ask her more questions?"

"She hadn't seen anything. At least we found out the killer drove a car. And that she didn't know the postman's name. If she had, she wouldn't have referred to him as 'the postie.'"

I buttoned my coat. Even at the warmest part of the day, in winter, the sun was pale, and even more so with the light cloud.

We knocked on the nearest neighbouring doors, but there was no answer.

At this time of the day, most people would be at work, which meant few or no witnesses. After a few minutes, we returned to the car and sat inside.

"One issue we'll have with this investigation is that we'll be a step or two behind the police, like now. If we're going to find an angle for you to write about, it must be something they've missed. Also, I think you should go to the press conference that O'Toole mentioned. They'll release the victim's details then."

"All right. What are you going to do?"

"I will visit the NZ Post mail depot and find out anything I can about the postal worker on this route today."

"Cool. But I'll come with you. It's only two thirty. I've got loads of time to get back for the press conference. Besides, my Vespa's at your place. I need a lift from you."

"I work better alone." A sense of déjà vu passed over me. I was sure it wouldn't be the last.

"I'm coming with you anyway. But out of interest, why do you think you work better alone?"

"Fewer arguments, for a start."

When I had worked at the detective agency, if I'd said something like that to one of my partners, they might have socked me one. But Deepa just threw her head back and laughed, then turned to me with a broad smile.

"If I wanted a peaceful life, I wouldn't be a reporter, would I?"

Chapter 4

THE NZ POST DEPOT was in the Northwest Side by the still-functioning airport, a half-hour drive from Crashmere. Roadworks peppered the route. Occasionally people were working on them. My Swift bounced over plenty of potholes and cracks on the way. It's impossible to avoid them all.

At the depot, I showed my ID, and the receptionist called the manager. We met with him in a compact meeting room with windows overlooking the broken-up car park. An art print on the wall showed a vibrant city night scene from some unidentifiable place. It wasn't Quake City

We sat around a small table. I didn't bother taking my hat and coat off.

Dave, the manager, was about my age. A ring of grey hair clung to his head below a bald dome. Worry lines creased his forehead and looked like permanent fixtures. Perhaps they were because of the stress of organising the mail delivery for a city beset by earthquakes.

I asked him for the name of the postman who had the route that included the street of the crime scene, hoping he didn't yet know that role was now vacant.

"That's Ricky Cohen. Why are you asking? Is he in trouble?" His hands trembled.

Obviously, he hadn't yet been told about the murder, and I wasn't about to break the news. "I'm making enquiries on behalf of a client." Stock answer. "Can you tell me about Ricky? Does he have any problems with anyone?"

Deepa kept her gaze on her notebook, following my lead.

Suspicion flashed over Dave's face. "Ricky's a decent guy. Friendly. Works hard. Never gets into trouble. He's never set a foot wrong as far as I know.

I can't imagine anyone has a problem with Ricky. Do you want me to call him?"

"Not right now. Any close friends here?"

"He gets on with everyone, goes out for drinks after work sometimes. Some of us watch the rugby together at the weekend. And he's married. His wife's name is…" He scratched his head. "Sorry, her name will come back to me."

"Never mind. Is there a desk or a locker or something like that for Ricky?"

"Yeah, a cubby-hole. Won't be anything in it except for his shoes and cycling gear. No one keeps any valuables in them."

I thanked him, and we walked back to the Swift.

Deepa thrust her hands in her jacket pockets. It was still cold. "He seemed anxious."

"Maybe his job is stressful." Or he's hiding something.

"What's next Danny?"

"Back to my office. You can pick up your wheels, and I'll find Ricky Cohen's wife. See what I can get out of her."

As I drove back to the main road, a police car passed us coming in. From within, Inspector O'Toole gave me a sullen look.

"What's his problem?" Deepa raised both hands in bemusement.

"O'Toole's? He's probably pissed that we beat him to Ricky's boss."

"Was that ethical, what we just did? Speaking to the victim's boss before the police?"

"About as ethical as investigative journalism." I grinned. I wanted to appreciate Deepa's broad smile again.

She obliged.

Maybe we'd get along okay after all.

Chapter 5

JOB DONE. It was fucking awesome seeing that guy jerking forward when the slug hit him. He didn't even realise I was behind him. He didn't suspect what was coming. Yeah.

Wait. He didn't know he was going to die. What would it be like if he had known? If he'd seen the gun? Seen me levelling it at him? Would he have begged for his life? Screamed? Peed his pants?

Nah, I didn't want him screaming, did I? Every fucking neighbour in earshot would have been peering out their windows.

I caress the smooth, cold metal of my shotgun, the stock, the barrel, the trigger guard. It's trustworthy. Dependable. Deadly. It's mine. I love the feel of it, its power. What I can do with it. What I did with it today.

Yeah, that guy jerked like a rag doll with a bloody rose blooming on his back when the slug hit him. Rockin'.

But I didn't see his face.

I frown. I wanted to see his face when I pulled the trigger, to see that fear in his bloodshot eyes before he died.

The next one will be different. He will get what's coming to him, what's been due for a fucking long time. He's going to know fear.

Fear was something I knew about. But I'm not Fear's bitch any longer.

Now I am the deliverer of Fear.

There are people who deserve to die. Bad people. Bad men who bring fear to others. I'm coming for you, assholes.

I stroked the gun, breathing hard. Then I rubbed myself with it until I moaned and shivered.

Chapter 6

I PARKED OUTSIDE my apartment building. It's a small one, six apartments in a brick-clad edifice marred with non-structural cracks, but only two of the apartments are occupied. Mine and the quiet but watchful Mrs Werther's, both up the first flight of stairs.

"I need a coffee before I go to the press conference, but it'll have to be quick. Can I come upstairs?"

"Sure. No problem."

We went upstairs and spent a couple of minutes passing pleasantries with Mrs Werther, who ambushed us on the landing. Inside my apartment, I made a cafetière for both of us while Deepa worked on her article. She downed the coffee in three gulps, said goodbye and left. Her Vespa roared into life and she rode away.

I was alone again. That's how I always worked, and how I usually lived. It's easier not to have to think of someone else, not to rely on them, not get hurt by them.

Torquemada brought me out of my nostalgic gloom when he brushed against my legs. He led me to his empty food bowl. I gave him a cup of cat biscuits and patted him for a minute. He purred, contented.

Torquemada was now the only company I had. Clara and I had split up years ago. This damned job didn't mix well with maintaining long-term relationships. I saw our daughter Lizzie as often as I could, but the hurt in her eyes when we parted was always evident. It pained me as much, but I didn't show it. If only I had more time to spend with her.

Burying my paternal guilt, I grabbed the voters' registry that I'd smuggled out of one of the earthquake-damaged libraries. I found Ricky Cohen's address. It was in Crumbledon. Not too far, then.

Minutes later, I parked outside a blue weatherboard house, strode up the path and knocked on the red wooden door.

A lady in a floral dress answered. "Yes?" She was brusque. Her auburn hair was pinned up high, and points of glitter shone from her copper eye-shadow.

"Are you Mrs Cohen?"

"No, that's my sister, Bernice. I'm Louise Slater. Look, this is an awful time. She can't talk right now."

I showed her my ID. "I know that Bernice's husband has been murdered. That's why I'm here. I'm helping the police." Did I say I was helping them? Must have been a slip of the tongue…

"She's already talked to them."

Another woman appeared to the side of Louise. She wore a red cardigan that matched the tint of red at the front of her otherwise greying hair. "Who's this?"

Louise turned to the other woman, whom I guessed was Bernice Cohen. "He's a private investigator."

"I won't take up much of your time." I expected to have to use the foot-in-the-door technique again.

"My sister doesn't want to talk to anyone." Louise started to close the door.

Bernice snuffled. "It's all right, Louise. Let him in."

I followed them inside and into an old-fashioned kitchen. Louise sat at a Formica table, but Bernice remained standing, as did I. Her eyes were red-rimmed. A purple bruise was visible below her left eye. Two partially filled wine glasses were on the table.

"Sorry for your loss, but I need to ask you about Ricky. Anything you can tell me might help catch his killer."

At the mention of his name, Bernice sobbed. "The police said he was dead. At first, I thought he'd crashed that new-fangled postal vehicle of his, but they said he'd been murdered. Shot."

"I know it's not much consolation, but Ricky died instantly." I kept my voice soothing. "He didn't suffer."

"But why would someone want to kill my Ricky? Why? Why?" Her words drew out in a cry.

"I hoped you could tell me that."

Tears flowed down Bernice's cheeks.

A lump rose in my throat. The last person I'd seen cry like that, uninhibited, was my grandmother on the day gangsters killed my parents.

Louise glared at me.

I hated putting Ricky's widow through this, but the first hours after a crime are crucial, and I didn't want to hang around and let any potential leads go cold. I needed to catch up with whatever the police had found out.

I spoke with as much empathy as I could muster. "Bernice, I understand how hard it is for you right now. I truly do. I've been there in your situation."

"You have?" She sniffled and stared at me.

"Yes, and back then I wanted justice." Though I never got it. I took a deep breath, then continued. "The same as I want justice for Ricky, to see the murderer behind bars where they belong. And to do that, I must move fast. Could you help me?"

"Okay." Sniffing back tears, she scrubbed her face with a tissue, then blew her nose. She sat back and crossed her legs.

"Did anyone have a grudge against your husband?"

Bernice shook her head.

"Was he involved in any illegal activity?"

"Of course not." She put her head in her hands, covering the bruise on her cheek.

Louise stepped between her sister and me, crossing her arms. "Bernice is too upset to answer more questions. I must ask you to leave."

Reluctantly, I nodded. "Thank you for your time."

Louise ushered me down the hallway to the front door.

On the doorstep, I paused. "How did Bernice come by that bruise on her face?"

"She walked into a door. This one, in fact." Louise closed it behind me with a sharp thud.

I drove back to the crime scene in Crashmere. Two constables were searching gardens in the street. The properties in this part of the city often had sizeable gardens, so it would take them a while. But it was now dusk, and they would give up any minute now. The nearby pubs would hold more attraction for them than poking around shrubbery in the dark and the cold.

I watched them until they returned to a patrol car and drove off. Thoughts of my parents being gunned down flooded my mind, unbidden, and my grandmother's endless tears leading to her premature death from grief.

My heart beat faster, the old pain flooding back. I pushed it away, focusing on my current case. Though Deepa had asked me to investigate, help her find background stories and come up with a psychological profile, I was already leaning toward solving the murder itself. I can't rest when criminals kill and walk away.

O'Toole and his team might find the killer, but I couldn't rely on that. I had to do it myself. I *needed* to.

Chapter 7

Day 1, evening

THE PRESS CONFERENCE would be over by now. From the comparative comfort of my car, I phoned Deepa. "Any news?"

"Not a lot. Victim's name confirmed, but we knew that. They have ruled out robbery. They're still looking for the murder weapon."

"Yeah, I'm at the crime scene, and I can see officers searching."

"Any hunches, Danny? I've finished the article for tomorrow's edition, but I can update it if you've got anything new."

"We don't have a lot to go on. No murder weapon, no leads, no motive. Either someone wanted Ricky Cohen dead or it was a random drive-by shooting."

"Okay, I get it."

I shuddered. "If it was random, and the murderer has kept the weapon, perhaps they plan to kill again. If so, O'Toole might finally have his serial killer. Let's hope that's not the case. But it's not the only plausible explanation."

"No? What are you thinking?"

"Gangs. Quake City's most notorious gang has sometimes used random murder to prove someone is ready to move up a level in the organisation."

"What, they just go out and kill someone to get a promotion?"

"It's happened before."

"And you're going to investigate if that's what happened today, aren't you, Danny?"

Someone has to. "Yes, and you're not. It's too dangerous."

"I want to come with you."

"No, it's too risky. I don't know what I'll find or what I'll do, but I don't want you along, putting yourself in danger."

"I'm still coming."

"No, you're not. I'll call you later." Assuming the gang don't catch me spying on them.

I disconnected to end the argument and drove off, steeling my nerves for the task ahead.

The Gruesome Crew had their headquarters in Swampside, over in the blighted east side of the city. An assorted bunch of organised thugs who made their illegal living from robbery, theft, pushing drugs, demanding protection from legitimate businesses, and contracted assaults and murders. Antagonising them would be like poking a bear with a sharp stick. Not a splendid idea.

And I planned to walk right into their den.

I skirted the edge of the Red Zone. The houses became more run-down, the roads deteriorated even more. Diversion signs were frequent to avoid the worst-damaged roads that doubtless no one would ever repair. Along one, I passed an abandoned car half-submerged in a sinkhole.

The gang's headquarters were along a darkened road where none of the streetlights worked. They'd probably smashed them. Moonlight and starlight provided a dim yellowish light that the gang couldn't snuff out. I parked two houses distant.

A light shone through my car's back window, and I ducked out of sight. A motorbike or scooter went slowly past and turned the next corner.

I waited a few moments, then sat up. No one in sight.

I got out of the car and paused, uncertain. Should I leave it unlocked for a quick getaway, or lock it to deter thieves? Would my car still be there in a few minutes? Were the gang's neighbours as bad as them? Maybe the neighbours had all moved away.

I left it unlocked.

My shoes were silent on the greasy road. Rain had fallen in the area in the past few hours. I crossed the road and approached the Grues' property. Loud rap music blared from inside. Good. They wouldn't hear me coming.

If the Grues had killed Ricky Cohen so one of their members could earn a promotion, they'd be celebrating tonight. I wanted to find out. That meant I had to get inside the property, if not the house itself.

A tall wooden fence surrounded it. Unscalable. I looked for another way and spotted a tree in the neighbouring property. Could I climb that and jump? No. Stupid idea. I might sprain my ankle, and even if I didn't, there'd be no way back.

I needed another option. But what?

The house next to the Grues' headquarters was dark. I sidled up the driveway, keeping to the fence line. Moonlight illuminated old wooden fence palings rotting in places or attached only by loose nails. I chose a place where one paling had already fallen off. With a bit of effort, I pried off the next three in line.

I slipped through the gap into the Grues' property and crouched in the fence's shadow, listening and allowing my eyes to adjust to the dark.

Nothing moved in the yard. Three cars were parked on the lawn. How many gang members were inside? At least three, but there could be a dozen.

I crept closer to the house, using the cars as cover. Still no one visible. I stood, ready to cross the lawn. The front door opened. A guy came out, smoking a cigarette. Moonlight glinted off the gang patch on his leather jacket.

I ducked down. Had he seen me? Would he sound the alarm, or stride over and collar me on his own? My muscles tightened with adrenaline.

Time to risk a peek. The gang member had undone his pants. His pee gushed forth over plants by the house. My nose wrinkled despite the distance. He zipped himself up and went back inside.

A minute passed. No one came out. I edged forward, then sprinted, head low, to the side of the house. I edged along, crouched low, silent in the sound of the rap music emerging from inside.

A windowsill appeared above me, paint peeling off it. I stood and peered over it into a living room. A music system sat on a table on the opposite wall, surrounded by bottles. Four Grues sat on old blue sofas, drinking and smoking.

I lowered my head. That didn't look like any kind of initiation ceremony. Maybe there wasn't one at all. Or maybe it hadn't started yet.

A dog barked. Then two barked together. Sounded like they were on the other side of the house. Chained up, hopefully. Had they caught my scent?

If I could hear the dogs barking, the gang members could too. And they might investigate.

I backed out from under the window and stood. Time to get out of here.

The cold, hard steel of a gun barrel pressed against the back of my neck. I froze.

A hoarse voice growled. "Who the fuck are you?"

Chapter 8

I TURNED SLOWLY, my heartbeat echoing in my eardrums, my jaw clenched so tight that I couldn't answer him at first.

A shotgun barrel was so close to my face that I couldn't focus on it without going cross-eyed. I fought a rising panic and found my voice. "I thought this was a friend's house."

The man with the gun scowled. Tattoos circled his facial features, and smoke swirled from a cigarette dangling from his mouth.

"You sayin' you're lost?"

I nodded, not taking my gaze off him. The guy was dangerous, but was he unstable? Jittery? Would the gun go off in my face? I suppose I'd never know if it did.

"Liar. Who are yer?"

Could I wrest the gun from his hands before he fired it? I strained with the thought. It might go off anyway…

The gang member kept the gun steady, the barrels pointing straight between my eyes. "Who the fuck are yer? Yer don't look like yer from another gang. What d'ya want here?"

I had no answer. I took a deep breath, dodged to the side, then barged him. The Grue slammed into the wall of the house.

I grabbed the shotgun by the barrel, but he wouldn't let go. We wrestled with it between us while he launched a tirade of expletives.

I stamped on his foot with my heel. He howled. I dropped low, rolling back, twisting, pulling him off balance. He crashed to the ground beside me. I spun over and smashed my fist into the side of his head as he tried to get up. He crumpled.

Now I had the gun. A Remington 12-gauge pump-action shotgun.

Footsteps. I swivelled to see the danger. Someone knocked me sideways. A metal chain swung over my head. The assailant pulled it tight around my neck.

I dropped the shotgun, gasping. My eyes bulged as I struggled for air. I clawed at the chain, trying to get my fingers underneath the links. They bit into my skin. My throat burned like I'd swallowed burning coals.

I kicked backwards with one foot, but my kicks were too weak. The brute had tugged my head back onto his chest. His grip tightened.

I would die here, strangled. The police would find my body in my torched car down by the Waimak river or rotting in the Red Zone somewhere. Or they might never find it.

There was a thud. The chain loosened and fell away, clinking in a pile on the earth. I fell backwards, gasping for air. My attacker was on his knees, slumped over.

Deepa stood by me, holding the shotgun like it was a club. "We need to get out of here, quickly. Get up."

I grabbed her outstretched hand, gulping mouthfuls of air. The guy I'd punched was stirring. And more of the gang might arrive at any moment.

Deepa took off across the lawn, half-dragging me. She was a runner; I wasn't, and I was wheezing.

When I stumbled, she pulled me up. We swerved around the gang vehicles and headed for the gap in the fence.

Shouts came from behind us. Angry, vengeful voices. Then barking.

Deepa slipped through the gap into the bordering property. I stepped through after her.

I turned my head. The barking sounded closer. "They've let the dogs loose!" My vocal cords ached, and I was panting.

We reached the road and started to cross. Deepa's scooter wasn't in sight. Had she come by taxi, or hidden her Vespa somewhere? Or maybe someone had stolen it.

I stumbled again, out of energy and short of breath, and dropped to one knee on the asphalt.

The dogs scrabbled at the gap in the fence. I looked behind. Two of them burst through and charged, barking ferociously. Pit bulls. They could tear us to pieces.

Deepa pulled me to my feet with a strength that surprised me and shoved me at the car. She vaulted onto the bonnet and slid across, while I yanked open the driver's door.

I slammed my door shut. Deepa got in her side moments later. She still had the shotgun.

I fumbled in my pocket for the car key.

A canine mouth with bared teeth appeared at the window. Wild eyes stared at me while paws scrabbled on the car. Both dogs barked fiercely.

Deepa shouted and grabbed at my shoulder. "Hurry!"

I jabbed the key into the ignition, turned it and jammed my foot on the accelerator. The Swift shot forward, leaving the dogs behind. They chased us for a few metres before giving up.

I swerved around the corner. "We made it. Thanks. You saved me back there." I felt my neck. In the sunshade mirror, I could see a bruise already forming.

Deepa looked through the rear window, then directly at me. "I said I'd be your back-up, didn't I? Now, let's get out of here."

After a minute or two, I was sure we weren't being followed.

"How did you get to the Grues' headquarters?" It was painful to talk.

"Taxi. I told the driver to wait for me."

"I didn't see anyone."

"No, he must have thought better of hanging around that area and left. What did you find out in there?"

"I didn't see much before they caught me. I got nothing."

She gestured. "You got this shotgun."

Chapter 9

Day 2, morning

DEEPA ARRIVED AT MY OFFICE at nine a.m. the day after the shooting. My door was already unlocked, and she entered, bearing two takeaway cups of coffee and a paper bag. I was at my desk, reading her piece in the *Richter Mail*, which described how a sharp private detective was helping the police, pursuing every clue and interrogating witnesses with finesse. It took me a moment before I realised she was referring to me.

Deepa opened the mouth of the bag, revealing two blueberry muffins. "Have you eaten? I brought you a muffin just in case."

"Thanks." My stomach rumbled. "Good article."

"The editor said he'll run another one when I come up with fresh material. The staff reporter duly reported the facts, as I told you they would. I'm going after something more personal. I thought today we could find out more of the victim's story."

"All right." I took a bite of the muffin. Delicious. "So, when do you get paid for the article?" Half of the money was due to me, and then I could buy my own muffins.

"It'll be the middle of next month. That's their payment cycle."

"That's weeks away." I sprayed crumbs onto the desk. "You didn't tell me it'd be that long."

Torquemada leaped up onto the desk and sniffed the largest crumb, as if sensing he and I might both be reduced to hunting for scraps if I didn't get paid soon.

Deepa smiled and leaned forward to pat my little companion. "Who's this?"

"My cat, Torquemada. I rescued him from a murder scene. There was no one to look after him. He was scrawny and fearful when I got him, but he's much happier now."

"Torquemada? Why did you name him after the Grand Inquisitor of the Spanish Inquisition?"

"Because he raked my hands with his claws when I brought him home for the first time." I coughed, embarrassed. "I may have overreacted."

"You think?" She stared at me with disbelief.

I sipped my coffee. It was hot and sweet. How did she know I liked it that way?

Torquemada curled up on my closed laptop.

My phone rang. O'Toole. I put him on speakerphone. "Good morning, Inspector."

"What do you think you're playing at, Ashford? The daily rag says—let me quote—'A sharp Quake City private detective is on the case in the pursuit of justice for the grieving postman's widow.' Remember, this is *my* investigation. The article barely mentions the police at all. What the hell was that reporter thinking? Negligent, if you ask me. And you, 'sharp'? What's that about?"

I ignored that. "Any luck finding the murder weapon, Inspector?"

He groaned. "No. We gave up searching when it got dark, and this morning the superintendent reassigned the resources elsewhere. I reckon the killer kept the weapon to use again."

"Serial killer, you think?" There was no evidence for this, but that wouldn't stop O'Toole leaping to that conclusion.

"If you were as sharp as that article made out, you'd see that for yourself, Ashford."

Deepa gave a wry smile.

"Do you know what the weapon was, Inspector?"

"Forensics report came back this morning. The perp used a 12-gauge shotgun. Ammunition was a lead slug."

I'd already worked that out. "Thanks for sharing."

"Yeah, well, it'll be public knowledge soon."

"I'll let you know if I find anything important, Inspector. Have a good day." I disconnected.

Deepa tilted her head. "Could that shotgun we took from the Grues be the murder weapon?"

"Maybe, or they might have another one. The problem is guns like that are commonplace."

"Right." She frowned.

"Our first stop will be Bernice Cohen's house. She was in too much shock yesterday to be of much help. Hopefully, something might have come to her overnight."

"Can we check Ricky Cohen's bank account for anything suspicious? Maybe he was being blackmailed and didn't pay up, or had gambling debts or something."

I shook my head. "Private investigators can't access that information. I only have the same rights as any ordinary citizen."

"Oh. I didn't know that. Damn."

I glanced at my watch. "Let's go. With some gentle questioning, we might learn something about Ricky Cohen indicating why someone wanted to kill him."

"And, hopefully, some details of his life that I can work into my next article."

"I've just thought of something. Let me make a call before we go." I picked up the phone and called the NZ Post Depot.

"Hello?" Dave's voice sounded strained.

"Dave, it's Danny Ashford here, the private investigator. I have a question for you." I jabbed the speakerphone button so Deepa could hear too.

"Make it quick, Danny. We're short-staffed with Ricky gone. And another of my guys didn't turn up to work this morning and isn't answering his phone. I'll have to deliver the post on his route myself."

My brain tingled. Another missing postie? "Okay, I'll be quick. Was Ricky enrolled in the KiwiSaver scheme? Did he have a life insurance policy through work?"

"Yeah, both. I did the paperwork for those yesterday. Two times his annual pay for the life insurance, KiwiSaver savings at the top rate since its inception, and a superannuation fund before that. He worked here for thirty-five years, so it'd be a tidy sum all added together."

"Thanks, Dave." I disconnected.

Deepa inclined her head. "That money will go into Ricky's estate. Does his wife get it, do you think?"

"Yes, she will do, because they have no children."

"I can't imagine her shooting her own husband, going home and then pretending to be the weeping widow when we arrived."

"No, she looked genuinely upset. I'm just trying to cover all the bases."

We put on our coats, I grabbed my hat, and we left. "You drive." I tossed Deepa the keys to my car. Being a passenger would give me time to reflect on the case.

But Deepa had other ideas. "Last night was scary. Do you think the gang knew who we were?"

I shook my head. "No, it was too dark. Neither of those guys saw you, and they're probably too lazy to figure out who I am." And too dumb.

Deepa took a right turn without remembering—or maybe without bothering—to indicate. "Good." She swerved into Crumblo Street heading south and accelerated past the ruins of a row of shops in old terraced buildings. "I want to ask Bernice Cohen some questions for an article."

"You talk a lot. And you're speeding. Slow down a bit, all right?"

"Sorry." She complied, then glanced at me while switching lanes. "Talking is part of my process. It's how I think through situations, judge people's characters, decide what's important… everything, really."

"I get it, Deepa. You talk to work things out. I work things out and then talk. It's taking me a while to get used to having you tagging along."

"I wouldn't be much of a reporter if I sat at my desk."

I sighed.

Chapter 10

WE DREW UP OUTSIDE Bernice Cohen's house in Crumbledon. Her sister Louise answered the door after my second knock.

"Is Bernice at home? May we talk to her?"

Louise glowered at us for a few moments, then showed us into the kitchen. The linoleum was grubby, unloved. Bernice sat at the small table, nursing a cup of tea, eyes drooping as if she had slept poorly last night, the bruise still visible. From the living room came the unique sound of a cuckoo clock striking ten.

"Sorry to bother you again, Mrs Cohen. How are you holding up?"

"About as best as could be expected. Can I offer you both a drink? Tea? Coffee?"

It was always hard to turn down coffee, and it would give me two or three minutes to have a look around. "Yes, please. Coffee, milk, three sugars."

Deepa gave a weak smile. "Black coffee for me."

I whispered in Deepa's ear after Mrs Cohen turned to get cups. "Keep her talking." She nodded.

I moved through into the dining room, browsing. What were the Cohens like? Art prints and a photo of a local cricket team with a younger Ricky Cohen decorated the walls. Double sliding doors led to the living room. A large flat-screen TV dominated one wall. There were no bookcases anywhere. How can anyone live without books?

A china cabinet held several minor treasures: fancy cups and saucers, and two sporting trophies for Ricky. Certificates in frames hung on the wall, all for Bernice Cohen: naturopathy, acupuncture, amateur dramatics society, local walking group 'Gold' membership.

"Oh, there you are. Coffee's ready." Mrs Cohen peered around the door. Her voice was monotonic, her expression flat.

"Thank you." I followed her back into the kitchen. "Mrs Cohen, how was your relationship with your husband?"

"What an odd question. Why do you want to know that?"

"It's just routine."

"Well, I would say it was like that of most couples who have been married a long time."

Deepa interrupted. "Were you still happy together?"

"Of course. Why wouldn't we be?" She sniffed. "Oh dear, I was trying to put this out of my mind for a while, and you come around asking ridiculous questions…"

"We wanted to assure you we're doing all we can to help you. Sorry for the invasive questions. We want to learn about Ricky and understand what was going on for him."

Bernice nodded.

I sipped my coffee. It was awful. Weak, lukewarm and she'd forgotten the sugar. I put it on the table. "Is there anyone we can speak to about anything out of the ordinary Ricky might have been doing in the past week or two?"

"No. Ricky wasn't doing anything unusual. Why are you asking these questions, Mr Ashford? The police already asked that."

"I'm following my own line of inquiry. The police don't always get it right." But she seemed to be telling the truth, or at least believed her husband wasn't up to anything untoward.

Deepa took out a notepad. "Mrs Cohen, can you tell me something about Ricky? I'd like to write about him."

Bernice turned towards her. "Like an obituary?"

"Yep. What did he do in his spare time? Clubs? Sports? Hobbies?"

"He played or watched sports most Saturdays." Her mouth turned down, then her eyes moistened. "Otherwise we were homebodies. Though we'd planned a holiday for the spring…"

Deepa made notes. "Do you have a photo we can borrow?"

"Yes, certainly." Bernice stood and went into the living room, returning after a few moments with a small framed photograph. "You asked about hobbies. Ricky often pottered around in the garage while I looked after the garden. He had a workshop there."

"Mind if we look?"

"Go ahead."

"I'll show you." Louise beckoned for us to follow her. It was an internal access garage, big enough for two cars. A Suzuki Swift, a more recent model than mine, took up one side. On the other was a workbench equipped with tools.

"Ricky made birdhouses and sold them on Trade Me." Louise gestured at several on the workbench in various stages of completion.

Four finished ones lay at one end. I took a closer look, admiring the designs. "Good workmanship."

Deepa took several photos with her phone. "Cool. This'll be great for my article."

I spent a few minutes checking cupboards, drawers, and a filing cabinet while Louise looked on. Nothing stood out, and I didn't have any more questions. There was no obvious motive for someone to want Ricky Cohen dead.

"I think we should leave you in peace. We'll be in touch." I doffed my hat.

We walked down the driveway instead of returning through the house. Louise followed us to my old car. "How's the investigation going?"

"I'm following up a number of leads." Standard answer.

"Thanks for the update." She turned and strode to the house.

Once in the car, Deepa grabbed my arm. "A number of leads? You mean zero. We've got nothing to go on."

"Zero's a number. Besides, we needed more information about Ricky to find out if there was a motive for someone to kill him. We've got nothing else and pursuing that is sort of like a lead."

"Sort of. Ha ha. Okay, then. Hey, I've just thought of something. We could check the gun register, see who owns a shotgun and go talk to them."

I stared at Deepa. "You actually want to solve this, don't you? Not just write background stories?" But did she have to follow me around? I'd do better on my own.

"Well… if we did, I'd have the jump on every other reporter."

"But why investigate a murder? Why don't you keep writing about whatever it was you were writing about before?"

She raised her chin. "I wanted a fresh challenge."

"Well, you've got it with this case."

She regarded me with her deep brown intelligent eyes. For a moment, I was almost lost in them.

After a few moments, she spoke again. "What's wrong with checking the gun registry, then?"

"Well, there's about two hundred thousand people registered to have a gun. That's plenty. But there's estimated to be over a million guns around. Shotguns don't even have to be registered in Quake City, and it could have been a stolen weapon or one sold illegally. The registry is next to useless."

"Shit."

I smiled. At last, a reaction I could appreciate.

"What's so funny?"

"Nothing."

Deepa leaned forward as if she'd just thought of something. "Most murder victims are killed by someone they know, aren't they? And Ricky Cohen socialised with his workmates. Let's interview them. Maybe someone will act nervous and give themselves away."

"We could do that for now." Though it's a long shot.

"Why 'for now'? What are you thinking, Danny? You still thinking about the gang?"

"Yeah, it could have been them. But it might also be a totally random crime by someone else. A quiet, middle-aged postman with no enemies is gunned down in cold blood, seemingly without provocation." Like my parents were gunned down. I gritted my teeth.

Deepa gazed out of the window. "Like one of those American drive-by shootings. The victim chosen at random."

"Exactly. We have to catch the murderer quickly. He or she might have acquired a taste for killing."

She whipped her head around to face me. "Do you think a woman could have done this?"

I shrugged. "Statistics say men usually carry out crimes like this, but you never know."

Chapter 11

Day 2, afternoon

I HAVE A GUN. It's a big gun. Why do I have a gun?

I throw it to the ground.

Is this a park? Can I play here? No, it's not a park. There are trees and bushes around me. Where am I?

Oh, look at that. There's someone here. He looks dead. Is he dead? He isn't moving.

Wow, it's him. *Bad man. Bad, bad man. Why is he here? Good that he's dead. He's a bad man. He won't come to the house no more when Daddy is out. He won't come in my room.*

Friendly bit bad man because bad man kicked Friendly lots. Good Friendly. But then Friendly had to die. This man said so. Now the bad man is dead too. He can't hurt me anymore.

My head hurts...

I pick up the gun and return to the car. Enough of this shit. Time to get the fuck out of here.

Chapter 12

Day 2, evening

WE SPENT THE AFTERNOON tracking down and questioning Ricky Cohen's workmates. Most of them were out delivering the mail, so it took time and used up a lot of petrol. They all said Ricky was a well-liked guy. No one knew, or said they knew, of any financial difficulties, enemies, or anything that might give someone a motive to kill him. Unless any of them were lying, it was a dead end.

In the late afternoon, we agreed to give up for the day. Deepa told me she would go for a run after she got home. I dropped her back at her scooter, then drove to Clara's house in the Northwest Side.

My ex answered the door. "You're late."

"Sorry. I was busy with a case."

She leaned on the door, frowning. "Thought you might be."

I changed the subject. "How's school?"

"I have a lot of papers to mark this evening. Thanks for taking Lizzie out."

Lizzie raced up to the door, her favourite stuffed toy, an owl called Twit, bundled in one arm. "Daddy!"

I got down to one knee and grabbed her as she leapt into my arms.

Clara smiled. "Someone's pleased to see you. Going anywhere nice?"

"Are we, Daddy?"

"Out to dinner, Lizzie."

"Yay!"

Lizzie, Twit and I got in the car, and I asked Lizzie where she wanted to go to eat. She had a few favourites. Fortunately, they were all inexpensive. Most had burgers on the menu too.

We ordered our food, sat down, and Lizzie told me all her school news. I tried to follow the complex relationships of her Year 5 class, but I couldn't concentrate and I soon became confused by all the alliances and betrayals amongst the nine-year-old girls. Give me a decent murder to solve any day.

Our food and drinks arrived. A sloppy burger for me, chicken nuggets and chips for Lizzie. Twit, sitting on the next chair, had nothing, but watched the proceedings with large glassy eyes.

Lizzie stared at me with a frown. "Are you listening, Daddy?"

"Yes, I am, sweetie. I just have an important case on my mind."

She gave an emphatic nod. "When I grow up, I want to be a private dick like you."

I spluttered my coffee over the table. "You mean a 'private eye' or 'private investigator', Lizzie."

She drank some of her juice. "If you say so."

"Private investigators don't always earn a lot. It can be dirty work, too. And sometimes you get shot at."

"You mean people shoot at you when you go through their rubbish?"

"Well... no. Usually not at the same time."

Lizzie jabbed a chicken nugget with her fork. I took a bite of my burger. At these family restaurants, the burgers weren't the same quality as those at Quake Burgers.

"Are you working on the postie case?"

I almost choked on some bacon. "How do you know that?"

She grinned. "I didn't. But now I do. Have you solved it yet, Daddy?"

"Not yet, but I will."

"I've changed my mind. When I grow up, I want to be a postie."

I groaned. Was she saying these things to aggravate me? Did Clara put her up to this?

No. She's nine. She's mastering the devious art of teasing her parents.

Chapter 13

Day 3, morning

IT WAS MID-MORNING on a dreary day. Drizzling rain beat on the window behind me. I was on my third cup of coffee and my second pastry. Deepa kept pace on the coffees but passed on the pastries, so I had to eat hers.

We were in my office, brainstorming while we ate. We had no fresh leads and needed a break in the case.

Deepa finished reading her article on Ricky in the *Richter Mail* and slammed the paper on the table. "The editor pared it back to half the original size. Not enough juicy details, I suppose."

"At least he published it." And we'll get paid.

Deepa's phone buzzed. She fished it out of her pocket. I shot her a glance while she read the message.

"Danny, we should go." She said grabbed my car keys from the desk. "That was an alert from the news desk."

Not an ordinary text message, then.

Deepa slipped on her jacket and scurried to the door. I followed, pulling on my raincoat and hat. In my haste, I didn't even bother turning off the lights.

Mrs Werther stepped out of her room and ambushed us on the landing. She smirked. "Good morning, you two."

"You seem pleased about something." I edged towards a narrowing gap between my neighbour and the bannister. It closed before I got there.

"Sorry, we're in a rush. News waits for no one." Deepa dashed past Mrs Werther on the other side. I tipped my hat and smiled an apology, then hurried after Deepa.

Mrs Werther's voice echoed down the stairs, wishing us a marvellous day together, as I followed Deepa out of the building and to my car.

"What's happened?" I slid into the passenger seat. She still had my keys and had already started the engine.

Deepa accelerated down the street and took a left turn without slowing measurably. Was there a special driving school for reporters where they taught them to drive like maniacs?

"We've got to get to Holemorton. A pensioner's been killed."

Deepa was speeding again. The accelerator and sharp steering were her prime focus. The brake seemed optional. Indicators appeared to be a total mystery to her.

"What makes you think this latest killing is related to that of Ricky Cohen?" I hung on to the handhold above the passenger door.

"He was shot while delivering advertising material."

"Hell's teeth. Sounds like you're right."

We reached our destination, a suburban tree-lined street near a school. Two patrol cars blocked the road, so we stopped and got out. It was still drizzling with rain. A body lay on the footpath, a bunch of sodden junk mail clasped in his hand. Constables worked to surround the area with crime scene tape.

Other cars pulled up. Reporters to keep at bay. Crime scene investigators, SOCOs, to comb the area for evidence. More police, forensic photographers and the coroner would arrive soon. Two murders in three days was gruesome, and everyone would have two thoughts in mind—were the killings related? Would there be more deaths? I dreaded to think the answer to those questions was 'yes'.

Deepa exited the car in a rapid, fluid motion and raced towards the scene, her ponytail bouncing.

I followed a few paces behind. My heart raced and my breathing quickened. Because of a second body? A reaction to Deepa's errant driving? Or something else?

I caught up to her. "We need a closer look at how the victim was shot." We found a section the constables hadn't taped off yet and slipped through. I caught sight of Sam, a detective constable I knew, and slipped him fifty dollars as we strode towards the victim. He pocketed it and didn't stop us.

The body lay uncovered. Some of the Quake City police were less respectful, or lazier, than they should be. I grimaced. Were any schoolkids around to see this?

The victim was a white-haired man in his late sixties or early seventies. His eyes were closed, and his face wore a deathly grimace. The perp had shot him in the leg and in the side of his chest. The latter shot would have killed him. Blood pooled around his side, soaking his cardigan and worn jeans, mixing with a puddle of water on the pavement.

I clenched and opened my fists. The palms were sweaty, and my breathing was choppy.

Another senseless murder. Poor guy.

Deepa wasn't with me. I looked around. She'd backed away a few steps, her hand over her stomach, looking away from the body.

I went up to her and put my hand on her shoulder. "Are you okay?"

"I'll be all right. I–I'm not used to this."

"I know."

I turned back to the scene, trying to imagine what had led to this. My professional thinking kicked in. Was it the same gun, the work of the same killer? Random, or deliberate?

"Danny."

Deepa grabbed my sleeve. She pointed at a trolley, the kind elderly people sometimes use for their shopping, lying on the ground a few metres away, a gaping hole in its side. Regional newspapers and junk mail spilled out onto the pavement, some in tatters.

"And there." I pointed at a fence nearby. Three splintered white palings indicated another errant shot.

"A pensioner topping up his income with a paper run. Why would someone kill him?" Deepa's voice sounded unsteady.

"No idea." The idea was chilling. A harmless old man gunned down in cold blood for no reason. Was it the gang, a retaliation for my incursion last night? A terrible thought. Bile rose in my throat, burning, and I almost choked.

"Are you all right?" Now it was Deepa's turn to ask me.

"Yes." I wheezed.

"You know, I told you there was a deeper story involved. I sensed it as soon as I heard about Ricky Cohen's murder. First a mailman, and now someone delivering junk mail. I think Inspector O'Toole's right, you know. A serial killer is at work here."

I faced Deepa, my expression grim. "Let's not jump to conclusions." Though I'd already make a few leaps myself. "First, let's see if there's a connection between the two victims, once we know who this poor man is."

"And if there's not a connection?"

I took a deep breath and exhaled at a place that gave me time to think. "Could be someone crazy fancying themselves as a drive-by killer. In which case the perp will most likely want to do it again."

I looked around. This area wasn't as affluent as where Ricky Cohen was murdered. The houses were smaller, the cars older, the gardens less well-tended. A few people had come out of their homes to see what was going on. An officer was questioning a young man in cycling gear sitting on the damp footpath a short distance away. He'd propped his bicycle against a nearby fence. Helmet in one hand, he raked through his long hair with the other while the constable took notes.

We edged closer to overhear their conversation. The constable ignored us once I discreetly slipped another of my fifty-dollar notes into his pocket.

"What colour was the car?"

"Black, maybe. The driver slammed on the brakes in the middle of the road a little way ahead. He leaned out of the car window with a fricken gun—a shotgun, I think—and fired several shots at the old guy doing his paper round. Then he drove off." The cyclist shook his head.

"Can you describe the driver?"

"Never saw his face. As soon as I saw the fricken gun, I stopped so I didn't cycle past."

"But you're sure the driver was male?"

"Maybe, but I'm not sure. Could have been a man or a woman."

The constable thanked the cyclist and directed him to an ambulance, where they would assess him for shock. I couldn't question him yet, but the guy had struggled to answer the constable's questions anyway following that scary experience.

"What now?" Deep sighed and looked at her feet. "I need something to write about. Maybe I could find some background information on the victim once we know who he is."

I faced her. "Deepa, show some compassion. This man was killed less than an hour ago."

"I'll make sure compassion shines through in my writing."

That was cold. I was staring at the poor victim's body, feeling sad for his family and friends. Deepa was merely planning how to make an article sound empathetic.

Deepa must have seen something in my reaction. "I do care, Danny, but I've got to be professional, otherwise I can't do my job. You're the same. So don't judge me. That's not fair."

She was right. "Okay. Let's get to work." I looked around. Among the few onlookers was a woman who had stood at her gate the entire time we'd been there, arms folded, looking unperturbed by the situation. She appeared to be in her fifties. Her house was at the edge of the cordoned-off area.

I strode over and showed her my ID. "Did you see anything, madam?"

"Not a lot. I heard what I thought was a car backfiring three or four times. I looked through the lounge window and saw Gary lying on the ground."

"Gary?" Deepa had caught up with me.

"Gary Smith. He's a local. I knew him slightly from church."

I took up the questioning. "What about the car? Did you see that?"

"I saw a dark-blue station wagon speeding away."

"Dark blue?"

"Yes. Definitely dark blue."

I frowned. The cyclist had said black, but it's not unusual for witnesses to give contradictory accounts because of the stress involved at the time of the event. "Did you see the driver?"

"No, I didn't get a clear look."

"Even a partial description would be helpful."

She shook her head. "Sorry. Can't help you."

I thanked her, and we moved away so we could talk without being overheard.

"I'm going with the double murder angle for my article, and how the killer must be caught soon. These victims need justice. Readers will love that angle."

There it was again, that professional detachment. "And do you actually think the victims need justice, or only that your readers will resonate with that idea?"

Deepa stared at me, open-mouthed. "Did you not hear me a few minutes ago? I'd be no use to anyone crying and wailing. I have to be dispassionate to do my job well. But for your information, of course I want justice for the victims. That's the key reason I switched to this field of reporting, and why I came to you for help. Though now I'm asking myself why I bothered."

Her rebuke stung. "Sorry, Deepa. I get it. I apologise. It was a misunderstanding. We're still getting to know each other. Can we get back to work now?"

"All right." She huffed.

"Let's find out where the victim lived, and talk to his family if we can."

Inspector O'Toole was talking to the coroner near Gary Smith's body. I sent him a text, and when he'd finished with the coroner, he came over.

"Ashcroft. We've got a serial killer at work here, just like I told you." He beamed. "Shotgun again, same M.O.—a drive-by shooter."

"You're probably right, Inspector." Had to happen sometime, like winning the lottery on a blue moon. "I'd like to visit the victim's house if that's all right with you, speak to his family. After the police have interviewed them."

His eyes narrowed. "We haven't identified the victim yet. There were a few dollars loose in his pockets but no phone or wallet on him."

"The victim was a local man, Gary Smith. That lady there knew him." I indicated her.

"Is that so?" O'Toole's lip curled. He snapped his fingers at his sergeant, Amy Ling, a slightly built woman in her thirties. She came over, notebook out. "Gary Smith. Local man. Find out where he lives. Let Ashcroft have access. Doesn't hurt to have another pair of eyes looking. He might spot something."

I smiled weakly. The inspector's words came across as condescending, but that was his manner. We had a grudging respect for each other. Or at least he did for me.

I glanced at the ground, then up again, to give the impression that something had occurred to me at that moment. "It's important that the perp is caught quickly, Inspector, in case they strike again. Do you want some help on this case?"

The inspector stared at me.

"I'm looking into it myself, as you know, and you've already asked me to check over Gary Smith's house."

O'Toole nodded. "Well, Ashford, if you have the time to delve deeper..."

"Just for you, Inspector, I'll make time."

"All right, but make sure you report anything you find directly to me. This is my investigation."

"Of course. But I also need access to everything the police have." I stared at him.

"If you must." The inspector left us.

Deepa waited until he was out of earshot, then her eyes blazed. "You're working for him now? You're supposed to be working with me."

"But I am working with you. I'm merely taking advantage of an arrangement I sometimes have with O'Toole on cases of mutual interest." I smiled. Would that disarm her fury? "Look at it this way." I mirrored her words when she first persuaded me to work with her. "We'll learn whatever the police discover and we can question potential witnesses while their memories are freshest. That'll help immensely with your articles, won't it?"

Deepa relaxed. The benefits of us working on the inside were huge. She must realise that.

Deepa chuckled. "You'll 'make time', you said. It's not as if you have any other cases at the moment, is it, Danny?"

"It doesn't hurt to sound busy."

"Doesn't O'Toole see it as you interfering with his investigation?"

"He might, but—"

"You *do* have something on him, don't you?"

"Let's just say that it's useful for him to have someone on the outside who can bypass police procedure when necessary to get things done. And I'm sure the inspector wouldn't like the superintendent to find out about some of the things I've done for him. He wouldn't be where he is today without me."

"I get it. He owes you, and every time you help him out, he owes you more. And he has to help you out in return when you ask, whether he likes it or not."

"You got it."

"That's an unusual symbiotic relationship you got yourself into, Danny."

"One that I use to my advantage—and that of my clients—whenever possible. Just don't write about it, okay?"

Amy approached. "Right, I have the details." She tucked her phone into her pocket. "Gary Smith lived alone in a small rented flat three blocks from here. No wife or kids. Seems he was getting by on the pension and the few dollars extra from his paper round." She gave us the address and said she would meet us there.

Chapter 14

WE WALKED. It only took five minutes to get there, but we had to wait another twenty minutes for a police locksmith to turn up. In other circumstances, I might have picked the lock myself, but in the presence of the police sergeant I thought it best not to do that.

The locksmith let us in after jiggling the lock with two thin metal prongs.

A musty, stale smell emerged when we opened the door. We stepped inside to a drab room furnished with tatty chairs, an old TV, and a worn sofa. It was dark and cold. A scrawny cat lazily yawned at us from the sofa

"Amy, may I call the SPCA about the cat?" I hated the idea that the victim's pet might be forgotten in the aftermath of the murder.

"No problem, Danny."

Deepa and I moved through the living room into the kitchen. A calendar stuck to the refrigerator with magnets had dates circled and notes like 'Phone bill' and 'Electric' scrawled underneath. This man lived week to week.

The flat possessed only one bedroom. Amy searched that while Deepa and I looked through the kitchen drawers and cupboards for anything that might suggest a reason for someone to kill this unfortunate pensioner.

Afterwards, we compared observations, but we'd all come up with nothing. No obvious motive, nothing suspicious, nothing out of the ordinary.

"This will fit nicely with the inspector's serial killer theory." Amy rolled her eyes, but the grim set of her mouth suggested that she thought he might be right this one time.

We walked back to the crime scene and got into my car. I sat for a while, thinking. Deepa took out her laptop and started typing.

"What are you writing?"

"The serial killer angle, like I told you. I'm assuming a psycho committed these murders, like you said."

"That's not exactly what I said, Deepa. I believe the killer may suffer from severe mental illness or a personality disorder."

"Actually, the word you used was 'crazy.'"

"Slip of the tongue. But we should also look into other things, like associations between the two victims." Things that O'Toole might overlook because he's hellbent on determining the killer's M.O., if any, and predicting where the perp would strike next.

"You mean, like did they belong to the same sports club, or did they know each other?"

"Yes, those things, but also did they have any acquaintances in common? We might get a lead that way. You came to the right guy, Deepa. Tracking down information like that is my specialty."

"And mine." Her response started as a retort, then softened. "Except when it relates to murder cases."

"Good. Then together we can cover twice as much ground in the same time." If she's as good as she says.

"Danny, maybe I've put too much pressure on us by saying I want to catch the killer. That's unrealistic. I'm just a reporter. I should stick to writing stories. The victims' backgrounds. Your investigative process. A psychological profile. We can't expect to catch the killer. That's up to the police. O'Toole will do that."

"Don't count on O'Toole to get it done."

He probably won't catch them. O'Toole is stubborn and won't give up, but he isn't diligent and he isn't smart. He's in his position because competent police officers, like most other people with any brains and the means to get out, abandoned Quake City when the authorities left it to decay and ruin following the big earthquakes. And because I've helped him on a few cases.

Someone had to find the killer, and it would be me. Fast. If it was a madman at work, they'll strike again.

Soon.

Chapter 15

Day 3, afternoon

I HAVE ACCESS to the police databases without them knowing about it thanks to a well-placed bribe. I spent the early afternoon in my office trawling through some of those databases, while Deepa sat opposite with her laptop and combed through social media sites, online old newspapers and anything else that might give us some background into either victim.

There wasn't much. They didn't have criminal records. They didn't appear to know each other or belong to or work for any of the same organisations at any time. In fact, they had nothing at all in common apart from being dead at the hands of an unknown killer with no apparent motive in either case.

And we were almost sure it was the same gun involved in both murders—a shotgun—and the killer's shooting was too inaccurate for him to be a professional hitman or military-trained.

The police hadn't found the murder weapon after the second death either. Maybe the killer still had it. Maybe to use it again.

I took a swig of coffee, and a shudder rolled down my spine.

"All right, Danny?" Deepa glanced at me across the desk. She notices everything.

"Yeah. Coffee's got cold, that's all." I wasn't going to admit I had the shivers in front of her.

"It's still steaming."

"Never mind. Look, this is where we're at with the case. One murdered two days ago, another murdered today, no prime suspect—no suspects of any kind, even—and no clues apart from vague sightings of an old car that could be black or blue."

"So, what are you thinking?"

"A potential serial killer who's likely to strike again, and soon."

"And this serial killer could be anyone? How do we find them?"

Whatever I said would end up in Deepa's next article, for sure. "Most shootings are carried out by men. Most serial killers are men under thirty-five. Most strike close to home at first. I don't mean to say that our killer is *definitely* a male serial killer living locally, but it's most likely."

"Is that how the police will approach the case?"

"I doubt it. Don't write this, but O'Toole will have the few constables he can get assigned to the case going out questioning everyone with a record because he doesn't know any better. That's too wide a net. He'll never be able to interview everyone. And I'm not sure that's our perp at all. I think the killer is someone who's struggled in life and has suddenly snapped."

"So, someone with mental illness."

"Exactly. And something triggered them to act as they did. If we could figure that out, we might find them."

Deepa studied me for a while, pursing her lips. "You want to catch this perp too, don't you?"

"Someone has to."

"And that someone has to be you, does it? Our arrangement was only for you to gather information and outline profiles so I can write stories."

"Imagine the profile you could write if we actually catch the killer."

She tilted her head from side to side. "True. I want justice for the victims too, but why the pressing need to solve it yourself? Does it have something to do with your parents?"

"Let's just say I don't like seeing murderers get away with their crimes."

Deepa nodded. "I'm with you on that. But being at crime scenes makes it so much more personal. I hadn't realised it would be this challenging, so in-your-face."

"Murder's like that. You don't have to be involved. Go home and write your articles. I'll update you on whatever I do."

"Oh no, I'm sticking with you. In the news business, it's best to get it first-hand."

Trust her to say that. But I was getting used to having her around.

"So, where do we go from here?"

I tapped at my laptop. "I'll make a list of local people who have been hospitalised with mental illness following a violent episode. Not PTSD, though. Plenty of people have trauma following the earthquakes. Too many to follow up on. My hunch is that it isn't one of them."

"How can you access medical records? Aren't they confidential?"

"Not to the police. Not since the earthquakes, anyway. Security's lax in Quake City now. Besides, that information is available on the darknet for a couple of hundred dollars to anyone who wants it. Maybe even on social media for free."

"I see."

"The police have links to most of the government departments. I can get a list of dark-coloured station wagon owners too, and we can cross-check."

"Wow. That's useful." Deepa smiled, and a tingle ran down my spine.

"I can't access social media accounts, though."

"No problem. I can do that. Not all social media sites have end-to-end encryption. A young hacker I know gets me access to those on a pay-as-you-go basis."

I frowned. "That's illegal, Deepa."

"It helps fill out news stories. Besides, everyone knows their so-called private data with those sites isn't private, it's sold to other companies for advertising purposes. If I access it to write a news story, how could they object?"

"If you say so."

"It can't be any more illegal than accessing police databases using a stolen identity, can it?"

That stung. "I guess not."

I ran some searches on the police databases for owners of dark-coloured station wagons living within five kilometres of Ricky Cohen's murder.

There were hundreds of them. I filtered those against people who'd been hospitalised for mental illness and came up with what was still an extensive list. Who would have thought there would be so many? The statistics showed the numbers of mental health admissions had more than doubled following the earthquake and redoubled with the struggles Quake City went through to recover to something resembling normality.

"How's it going?"

I spun the laptop so Deepa could see the results. "There are too many people listed here. We will have to narrow it down more. Find the most probable suspects and hope we get lucky."

Without warning, Deepa reached over, took my hand and squeezed. "You don't have to do this, Danny. This is police work. Just come up with a psychological profile for me to write about."

"No. I'm going to investigate this fully. People are dying. The police are undermanned and under-brained. They need all the help they can get."

"But you're only one guy, Danny." She released my hand.

I raised my chin. "I'm the best private—"

"Yep, I've heard that before. You're still just one guy. I'll help you. Then at least there'll be two of us."

Somehow, I knew she'd say that. "It might be dangerous."

"From what I've seen so far, private detective work isn't any more dangerous than investigative reporting. You want to know why I keep in shape? It's so I can get away from angry people when I ask questions they don't want asked."

"All right. We're a team, then."

"We've already established that. Are you being sarcastic?"

"Not at all."

Deepa had another look at the list on my laptop. "We could concentrate on those people who had the longest stays in a mental hospital ward, or the most stays. As a starting point."

"Great idea."

Deepa printed the file. My old inkjet sputtered into life and disgorged several faded pages with the details we needed. I picked up a green highlighter pen.

"Give me that." Deepa snatched it from me. She fetched the printed pages, returned to the desk and browsed through them at speed, highlighting occasional rows.

"Here. All these people had stays of over three months, or four or shorter stays. But it's still a dozen people."

"That was quick."

She smiled. "I do a lot of word puzzles. I'm used to spotting patterns like this."

I glanced at my watch. "It's three thirty now. We might have time to interview a few of them before it gets late, but not all."

"Then let's split up. Take half each."

"Split up? No way. I don't want you coming across the perp on your own."

Deepa tilted her head. "I'll be fine. I can look after myself."

"It might be dangerous—"

"Who rescued whom two nights ago?"

I gave up. "All right."

We divided the names. Deepa grabbed her bag. I located my car keys underneath Torquemada, who was sleeping on the end of the desk. We left, passing the ever-watchful Mrs Werther, who gave me an exaggerated aren't-you-the-lucky-guy look that Deepa also must have seen, and went downstairs, Deepa to her scooter and I to my Suzuki Swift.

The heavy cloud darkened the day, and the drizzle had increased to a steady rain.

Deepa's phone buzzed and she called out. "Wait."

I paused with my hand on the door handle, chilled. Was that a news alert? Another murder?

Deepa rushed over. "We've got to get to Dumpsbury. Someone waved a gun from a car at a courier driver not five minutes ago."

"Anyone get the number plate?" There's always hope.

"No such luck."

We got into my car, and I started it. "Where exactly?"

Deepa already had Google Maps loaded. "The incident happened near a main road. Shit, the perp's probably already gotten away."

Ten minutes later, we pulled up by two patrol cars. Like Deepa had said, it was only a hundred metres from a main road, on the slope of a hill by a park. On the corner, a car lay half-buried under a collapsed wall, another reminder of the earthquakes that gave Quake City its name.

There was no cordon in place here. We scurried toward a Courier Post van parked across the footpath a scant distance away.

A young male constable stood questioning the Courier Post driver, a stocky woman who appeared to be in her forties. Her face was flushed. She held an umbrella.

The constable turned to us. Before he could warn us away, I showed my private investigator's ID. "I'm authorised to work on this case by Inspector O'Toole."

"All right. This is Liz Nicholls. She's all yours. I've taken a statement." The constable strode off to join other officers knocking on doors, looking for witnesses.

I turned to face the courier driver, trying to assess whether she was in shock. She seemed a little shaken, but not too bad for someone who had just undergone an ordeal like she had. "Liz, tell us what happened in as much detail as you can remember."

"I just told the officer there."

I hear this all the time. "We're working in parallel. If you wouldn't mind repeating it? You may even think of something else."

Deepa had her phone out, recording.

"Sure. I stopped here to deliver a package to this address. As I got out of the van, I noticed a car cruising up the street. Slowly, you know, that's why I took notice. I opened up the back of the van to get the package, but I froze when I noticed the car had stopped and the driver was pointing a shotgun at me out the window." She paused and took a deep breath.

Deepa spoke up. "Then what happened?"

"I just about shit myself. I couldn't move and I thought, well, I thought, Liz, this is the end, gal. Just like that poor postman I read about in the newspaper. But a moment later, the driver yanked the gun back into the car and sped off.

I was really shaking, I can tell you. It took me a minute to steady my hands enough to call the police."

We needed more than that to go on. A description would help. "Did you get a clear view of the driver?"

Liz shook her head. "No, I didn't pay much attention until I saw the gun—and then I couldn't look at anything else."

"Was the driver a man or a woman?"

"I can't say for sure. It was too shadowy and dark with these clouds. I didn't see."

Unfortunate. Though maybe Liz was too shaken up to recall details. "A sedan? Might it have been a station wagon?"

"Could have been. I'm not a hundred percent on that."

"And what time did all this happen?"

"It was about ten to four."

"Thanks, Liz. Are you going to be all right?"

"I might take the rest of the day off."

"Excellent idea. Thanks again."

We left Liz to the care of the waiting ambulance officers and returned to my car, splashing through puddles. Water ran off the brim of my hat as I bent to get inside.

Deepa slammed the door closed. "So, what's going on with the perp's car? She said it was a sedan at first. Do you think the killer's switching vehicles?"

"Maybe." I scowled. That would confound our efforts to find them. "Probably not, though. Our victim doesn't know what she saw. Her testimony might be unreliable. She doesn't know if the driver was male or female, or what the car was, because of the shadowy overcast conditions. All she was sure about was that they had a shotgun."

"Do you think it's our killer?"

"The perp used a shotgun both times, and the target was someone delivering letters or packages… My guess is it's the same perp because of those combined factors. Let's go with that for now."

"Okay."

"We need to ask ourselves the question: why didn't the perp shoot this time?"

Deepa tilted her head. "Maybe the perp didn't realise at first that their target was female. Maybe they only want to shoot men."

She's clever. "Could be. Men delivering the mail or packages. That's a niche group."

"So, should we be looking for someone with a grudge against people delivering things?"

"Yeah, that seems likely. Or it could be someone with mental illness or a personality disorder, who's hearing voices telling them to carry out these murders."

"How awful."

"Though another reason they didn't shoot might be that they've started to feel guilty."

"Really? Does that happen?"

"With someone crazy enough to drive around shooting postmen, who knows?" I sighed. "But I think the perp will be back in action soon. Regardless of why they didn't shoot this time, there's already been two murders. The killer won't stop until someone stops them."

We needed some luck. Badly.

Chapter 16

Day 3, early evening

DEEPA WENT HOME to write her article before the deadline for tomorrow's paper whistled by. I looked up directions to the first highlighted name on my list.

Roy King was in the garage at his home address, which was also his workplace. He worked for himself nowadays. That didn't surprise me. No one in their right mind would give him a job, not after jail time for a string of assaults and aggravated robbery. I'd known of him for years through the crime pages of the *Richter Mail*, and he'd come up on my search as he'd been hospitalised a couple of times with psychotic episodes.

I introduced myself.

Roy crossed his arms, set his jaw and leaned back against the black station wagon that interested me. "I ain't done it."

"I haven't accused you of anything, Roy. This is routine questioning."

"Yeah? Well, I don't know nuffink, either. And I don't know no one who knows stuff, neither. Got it? I'm clean now, got my own business and everyfink."

My brain raced to keep up with all the double negatives. "And what's that, Roy? Your business?"

"Extermination." He grinned. "I get rid of people's little problems."

My knees weakened. I forgot to breathe. Words failed me.

He pushed himself off the car and approached. I took a step back involuntarily. He moved to the side, revealing sign writing in bright yellow on the side of the station wagon. *SMIRKED–Spiders Mice Insects Rats Kockroaches Exterminated Dead.*

Pest control. Somehow, it suited him. "Cockroaches starts with a 'C'."

"Does it?" He shrugged and grinned. "Good money in pests. I went to Bali last month for me holiday."

Bali. And I wondered if I could afford a long weekend in Hanmer Springs. "You mind if I have a look in your car, Roy?"

"Nah. Go ahead. Whatever you're looking for, I ain't got nuffink to do with it."

I peered through the driver's window, then walked round to the passenger side and looked through that. The usual detritus that accumulates in cars was there in full force—soft drink cans, fast food boxes, gum wrappers, loose coins… but no shotgun.

"You mind popping the boot for me, Roy?"

He did that. An assortment of what appeared to be pest control paraphernalia assaulted my eyes and nose. It wasn't pretty and it stank worse. Could that conceal a gun? I wasn't keen to rummage around in there to find out.

"Thanks, that's all I need." I circled the car to view it from all angles. The stench of the pest control stuff—whatever it was—filled the garage. I almost choked. Maybe Roy had gotten used to it.

"About time you left. You're more of a pest than those rodents I deal with."

I ignored him and returned to my car. The rain had stopped at last.

I drove to the address of the second person highlighted on my list. It was a young guy suffering from antisocial personality disorder with a history of bar fights.

It turned out he lived with his mother. She was home, but he wasn't. She told me that she didn't know where he was, but he sometimes went to the West Coast for a few days, staying with friends. It was a believable story. There were plenty of bars over there, and locals itching to fight.

§

I went to Quake Burgers and ate one of their sloppy burger specials. That gave me some time to think about the case while I picked up lettuce and beetroot expelled from the burger.

O'Toole had nothing solid to go on, I was sure. Neither did I.

A wave of Imposter Syndrome hit me. What was I thinking, investigating these murders? That's police work. The police have more people, more resources, more time, even if the investigation is run by a dim-witted inspector. I'm on my own. Deepa asks more questions than she answers, and she's only interested in hitting her next deadline.

My line of work ordinarily involved finding people or things. Sometimes the people were dead, but I usually didn't investigate further. Anything beyond that was up to the police—if they did anything at all.

So, what made this case special? Deepa wanting me to construct a psychological profile of the killer so she could publish it? I'd read a popular book on forensic psychology, but that was the extent of my training on the subject. Did I know what I was doing? Did my assumptions make sense? Did *anyone's* assumptions make sense when there was a crazy person driving about shooting at postmen and couriers?

Apart from O'Toole, who had got it right this time.

When had I gone over that line from working on a profile to trying to solve the murders? What had pushed me to that? Deepa didn't expect me to do that. So… why was I?

Was it to impress her?

No, it couldn't be. Ridiculous notion. What, then? The idea that death could be so swift and random and unexpected and at the chaotic hands of a madman? The sense of the unfairness of it? The thought that the killer wielded the power of life and death over his victims by his twisted whims alone?

A mental image of my parents lying on the floor of a bank, shot dead by criminals who fled the scene, came unbidden to my mind. The blood pouring from my father's neck where a bullet had severed an artery. My mother, shot through the heart, lying on her back on the blood-pooled marble, glassy-eyed.

I sat brooding, watching other customers eating their messy burgers, feeling alone.

It was me against the killer. I had to find them. I had to stop them. Only me.

And Deepa. Though I'd always worked better alone, she wasn't too bad to have along for the ride. She noticed things, asked questions—many of them insightful—and she was earning us something for our efforts.

I shook my head, drawing nearby patrons' attention. What was I doing? I had no leads, no suspects, not even a description of the killer; only that he—or she—drove a dark-coloured vehicle. There was no obvious motive for the murders of Ricky Cohen and Gary Smith, nor anything obvious to link them together. Threatening Liz Nicholls this afternoon and not shooting was another piece in a distorted puzzle.

I'd found out nothing.

The sense of Imposter Syndrome swept through me like a tsunami through a house of cards. Call myself a private investigator? The best in my part of town, even? Sometimes I couldn't even find my cat. How was I going to find a merciless serial killer?

As if to emphasise my shaky self-confidence, a cracking sound came from the earth. The ground rumbled for twenty seconds, the salt and pepper shakers rattling on my table like castanets.

Yet another aftershock was striking Quake City.

It was only a little one. When it passed, I ate some more of my burger.

§

It was overcast and getting colder, now that the night had set in. It would rain soon. The gloominess echoed my mood as I drove to the address of the next person to interview on my shortlist: a woman. Even though the killer was statistically most likely a man, I couldn't rule women out.

Linda McKenzie lived in an old villa in Holemorton that had somehow escaped being bulldozed and turned into a group of retirement units. On the traditional quarter acre that is less common nowadays, her weatherboard house and garage stood in impeccable condition, as good as when they were built.

A navy-blue station wagon sat in the driveway. I peeked through the windows, but most of the interior was in shadow. The light from the nearest working streetlamp showed nothing incriminating. There wasn't much of anything inside. It was the cleanest car interior I'd ever seen.

McKenzie was on my list because she'd spent three months in a psychiatric unit after being put under the Mental Health Act for aggressive behaviour. From the looks of the garden and car, she had a smidgen of OCD as well. Following treatment and medication, she'd returned home.

I knocked on the door.

A voice called out after a few seconds. "Who is it?"

"I'm Danny Ashcroft, a private investigator. I have some routine questions for Ms McKenzie."

The door opened. "That's me. What's this about?"

I showed my ID. "I'm searching for the owner of a vehicle seen at the scene of a crime. Do you mind telling me where you were earlier this afternoon?"

Her eyes narrowed. "Why are you here? Am I under suspicion of something?"

I ignored the first question. "Not at all. I'm just helping out the police with general inquiries. It's routine. No one's under suspicion." Apart from everyone in Quake City.

She relaxed her posture. "I was here most of the afternoon, except when I delivered an antique clock that I'd finished fixing up. Got home about four o'clock."

"Where did you take it?"

She told me the name and address. "Would you like to see my work?"

"Sure."

She went to the side door of the garage, opened it and went inside. I followed. Someone had converted the garage into a large workshop. Benches stretched along the long sides. Neatly arranged tools took up one third of one side. A line of clocks and parts lay along the space.

No shotgun. No gun cabinet.

"I repair stuff like this. It's my business, lets me work for myself."

"Okay, thank you. I won't bother you any longer."

"Here's my business card in case you ever have a clock that needs fixing." She handed me a card with a business name and a corny picture of a cuckoo clock on it.

I bid her goodbye and returned to my car. I made the call to verify Linda's alibi. She had, indeed, delivered a repaired clock when she said she had. I checked the address on Google Maps, trying to figure out if she could have made a detour to attack Gary Smith. It wasn't impossible, depending on the route she'd taken and the traffic at the time.

Damn the ruined road cameras. The earthquake had destroyed some of them, and the others hadn't been maintained since because of budget cuts. In the pre-earthquake days, police officers would have combed through footage from cameras in the area to identify the car and track it. But it's not possible now, even if there were constables available to do it. And the chance of finding the car on my own was dismal.

§

I could question one more person from my shortlist before calling it quits for the night. Darkness closed in, wrapping its chill around me. I put the heater on in the car. I drove to the address of a young man with borderline personality disorder. The houses were smaller, the yards not so well-kept, the cars less enviable.

A light was on in the front room, and a TV blared. I banged on the door with my fist.

A middle-aged woman with large tattooed forearms opened the door. She puffed on a cigarette and stared at me.

I introduced myself. "Is Stephen Bishop here?"

She blew the smoke in my face. "No. I'm his mother. What d'ya want him for?"

I gave my now-familiar spiel and tried not to breathe in her smoke as she paid attention and listened.

The woman dropped her cigarette and ground it onto the step to extinguish it. "Stephen's in an acute ward at Holemorton Hospital. He went off his meds two weeks ago and self-medicated with synthetic cannabis. It didn't work out well for him."

"All right, thanks." I bid her goodbye, returned to the car and called the hospital to verify that he was there. They wouldn't tell me over the phone, so I had to drive there and show my ID to find out. He'd been there for five days, but they had allowed him out whenever he wished. They wouldn't give me any more details of his movements.

I drove home, my thoughts churning. Was Deepa right? Had the killer left the Courier Post driver alive because she was a woman?

The perp was operating to some twisted logic that made sense to them alone.

Chapter 17

Day 3, night

I LISTEN CAREFULLY, but I can't hear him now. He's quiet, or he's not here.

His behaviour's out of control. It's worse than ever. I don't know what he's done or what he's going to do, but I know it's bad.

He scares me.

I peer in the mirror and imagine him looking back at me. Cold and harsh. Determined and mean. Vindictive and murderous.

I turn away, shaking, and sit on the bed, hyperventilating. My chest tightens. My vision blurs. Nausea sweeps over me. A panic attack.

Breathe... breathe... breathe.

Eventually, it passes. I take deep breaths, fighting to regain some calm. He might come back anytime.

When he does, will he do something to me? Will he destroy me? What can I do to stop him, if he tries?

I can't get away from him. He can always find me.

I sob into my pillow for a long while.

Chapter 18

Day 4, morning

AFTER THE EARTHQUAKES, the authorities deemed some of the eastern part of the city unsuitable for buildings because the ground was too unstable. That's what becomes of creating a city on a marsh.

The houses and boundary fences were removed, but the roads and footpaths weren't. They live on as crumbling, pot-holed ghosts, barricaded from vehicles belonging to the public. Eerily, street signs point down them towards nothing of significance. The trees and bushes also remain, aligned along the former boundaries of private land where the houses once stood.

The Red Zone. It's a poignant reminder of what happened to the city. It's a pleasant place to take your dog for a walk. And it's a perfect place to dump a body.

At nine thirty in the morning, Deepa's phone alerted us that another victim had been found. Was it a third victim of the killer we sought?

We parked near the closest barrier and got out of the car. The morning was chilly, with drizzle threatening. Apart from a few remaining wisps, early morning fog had cleared. Across the damp ground we could see a woman with a dog on a lead was being questioned by a constable. Inspector O'Toole and Sergeant Amy Ling watched over SOCOs searching the area, and a constable stood at the barrier to prevent anyone from venturing closer.

Deepa peered through her phone's magnification app. "I can't see anything of the crime scene from here."

"We need to get in there. I'll call O'Toole, see if he'll allow us access now rather than waiting until the SOCOs have finished."

"How will you convince him of that?"

"Appeal to his vanity." I grinned and called the inspector.

He answered after the first ring. "Ashcroft. So, you've heard the serial killer has struck again."

"I heard there was another murder, Inspector. And you think it's the same serial killer?" I glanced at Deepa.

"Certainly. My years of detective work have given me a sharp eye for these matters."

"I understand, Inspector. I wish I had your perspicacity."

"You wish you had... what? Oh, look, never mind, I can see you at the barrier. Your hat's a dead giveaway. Tell the constable I give you permission to come over. I'll show you how a real detective gathers insights from a complex scene. Just don't trample any evidence."

"Thank you, Inspector, much appreciated." I disconnected, fuming. Toadying up to people was an essential skill in my job. I didn't have to like it, though.

"Arrogant ass." Deepa's assessment of the inspector was solid.

The constable let us pass, and we hurried across the patch of Red Zone to the crime scene.

Amy Ling met us and nodded towards the woman with the dog. "That's Ruby Coupp. Her dog found the body and she called it in. She didn't see anyone else around."

I glanced over. Ruby was about thirty, her face flushed from the cold or from the exertion of restraining her dog or both. Deepa switched on her phone's voice recorder, and we questioned Ruby, but found out nothing more.

We approached the bushes, now wild and uncontrolled, but once a well-tended part of someone's garden. Tyre tracks crossed a patch of soggy ground in front of us and led to a shrubbery, behind which there was a flurry of police activity.

I stopped and extended my arm so Deepa wouldn't step on the tracks. Ruby's dog hadn't been as careful. Paw prints overlaid the tyre marks.

"Looks like the killer drove around the barriers and right up here."

O'Toole emerged from the shrubbery. "There you are, Ashcroft." He glared at Deepa. "I didn't say you could enter the crime scene. This is confidential. The news briefing will be later."

I jerked my head towards Deepa and spoke to O'Toole. "She's my assistant." Deepa glared at me.

"Ah. Well... just don't write about anything that's not in the press briefing."

"I promise."

A reporter's promise. How much was that worth? "Do these tyre prints lead to the body?"

"Yes. The killer must have driven up here and dumped the body behind that shrubbery." O'Toole beckoned. "Come with me. I'll show you how I know it's the same killer."

We avoided the tyre prints and entered the shrubbery. A man aged about fifty lay there in an unnatural pose as if he'd been dumped like a worn-out sofa. He wore jeans and a cotton tee shirt, not enough clothing to be outside in this temperature. A gaping hole took the place of the upper right side of his head. A shotgun cartridge dangled from his mouth as if it was a metal cigar.

"Shit." Deepa succinctly stated her initial analysis of the crime scene. She recoiled, backed away and vomited into the bushes.

My stomach churned too at the grisly sight, but I was more used to it than she was. When I'd seen enough, I looked away, my legs weak, my heart palpitating.

O'Toole looked on, impassive.

"See the shotgun cartridge? That is what I wanted to show you, Ashcroft. It's a shotgun killing. Same *modus operandi*, same killer. Simple."

"Lead slug?" I struggled to regain my professional demeanour. Seeing the shotgun cartridge between the corpse's lips didn't help.

O'Toole nodded. "Yes. No way to determine if it's the same gun. I've taken the not-unreasonable view that it is."

And the victim, again, was male.

"Once again, we haven't found a weapon at any of the crime scenes, including here, or anything else left behind apart from the tyre print, though I'll keep the constables searching for a while."

"I don't understand." Deepa kept her gaze averted from the body. "I've watched crime shows on Netflix. Detectives on them can determine if it's the same gun."

Before O'Toole could snap at her, I explained. "Shotgun barrels aren't rifled, so they don't leave a pattern on the slug that forensics can compare with others. All we know is that it's 12 gauge."

"I see."

"Do you know who he is, Inspector?" My voice still sounded hollow.

"Not yet. There was no ID on the body."

"There's no blood splatter. The perp killed the victim elsewhere and brought him here later. Have you worked out the timeline yet?"

"The coroner is on his way to provide his first best guess for the time of death."

"Clothing's damp, maybe from the rain yesterday."

Deepa nodded. "Do the descriptions of any missing persons match this man?"

Good question. I'd been wondering that myself. Deepa was proving herself more and more insightful.

"I'll get the team on it." O'Toole probably meant he'd tell Amy Ling to find out.

The inspector took a step closer to me. Deepa, perhaps sensing he wanted to speak to me alone, or wanting to remove herself from the scene of the dead body, walked out of the shrubbery, leaving us alone.

"Have you got anywhere on this investigation yourself, Ashcroft? Do you have any leads?"

I shuffled my feet. "Not yet. I have a list of possibles—certainly couldn't call them probables—whom I've started questioning, based on a rough initial profile I came up with."

"I have nothing. No murder weapon, no suspects, no motive. Nowhere to start. This is undoubtedly the most cunning serial killer I've come up against. And the superintendent is demanding progress. She's breathing down my neck like a bad-tempered dragon."

"When you've identified this unfortunate man, Inspector, let me know. I'll search for patterns and try to build a more in-depth psychological profile of the killer. I suggest you do the same, and then we'll compare notes."

"I was hoping you'd say that."

"There must be something. The killer's not a ghost."

Though they were as elusive as one.

Chapter 19

Day 4, afternoon

WE LEFT THE SCENE and headed for a meal at one of the gourmet quakeaway places: burgers, chips and coffee, the traditional balanced meal of the private detective.

Deepa only ordered coffee. "How can you eat after seeing the giant hole in that poor man's head?"

I remembered to swallow before answering. "When I'm on a case, I have to eat whenever there's a chance, and eat quickly. I never know when I'll be on the move again."

She pulled her laptop out of her bag and started typing. "Want to make a statement on how you feel progress is going in your investigation, private investigator Danny Ashcroft?" She said my title and name teasingly.

"I'm pursuing my own lines of inquiry, and it's still early days."

"And unofficially?"

"We've got nothing. Don't write that."

She sighed. "I've got plenty to write. A third murder in four days is huge. It's time to invent a moniker for our killer. That'll pique reader interest."

"A moniker? Like what?"

"Something snappy. I need to think about it."

"Must you?"

"It'll engage readers, get them invested in the case. The more readers are involved, the more likely someone will come forward with information."

"Investigation by media, then." And more people will buy the newspaper too. Maybe that was a factor.

Deepa tilted her head from side to side without answering, the head bobble I'd seen several times before. Did it mean something, or was it merely a mannerism?

We talked about next steps. Deepa's scooter was at my office, so I said I'd drop her back there. She would write her article while I went to interview the next person on my shortlist. Deepa, it seemed, was too busy with her reporting work to start on her own list.

Some time later, I pulled up outside the home of Al Phillips, a young man who had once spent four months in hospital with a mental illness diagnosis.

Many of the southern suburbs were well-to-do areas for the socio-economically advantaged. Tornby was ten minutes' drive from the prime hills and foothills locations, and, while it wasn't all bad, parts of it were where those people who fell through the cracks of society might end up. There were plenty of actual cracks here too.

A dark blue station wagon sat parked on the front lawn of the old house. There was little in the way of planting. The property looked unloved and was probably rented. The entire place reeked of decay and many other unidentifiable stenches. I choked back bile and knocked on the door.

Al Phillips answered barefoot, his eyes red and pupils dilated, looking like he'd just woken up. I showed my ID, and he became more alert.

"What do you want?" He shoved the door wide open. It banged against the wall.

"I'm helping the police with some routine inquiries. Is this your car?" I indicated the old station wagon.

"Yeah, what of it?"

"Mind telling me what you were up to yesterday?"

"Nothing. Just hanging around. Sleeping, mostly."

"Sleeping in the day? Do you work at night?"

"Yeah. The owls sleep in the day, so I do, too. Then I can be awake for the night."

"Owls? What owls?"

"I do their work. The rubbish, the litter. I clean it up. The owls tell me where it is."

I ran my hand through the locks of hair poking out from under the front of my hat. "Let me get this straight: you sleep in the day and go out at night to pick up litter wherever the owls tell you."

"Yeah. They know where it is. Splendid night vision, owls."

"I didn't know we had owls living in the suburbs, Al."

"Of course not. They're not actually here, they're in the forests. They talk to me telepathically and they tell me where the litter is. I do their work. I clean it up."

I had to ask. "If they're not actually here, Al, how do they know where the litter is?"

He tilted his head to the right and stared at me for some time before he answered. "The birds here see the litter and fly out to tell the owls. The owls tell me where the litter is. I do their work. I clean it up."

Al seemed intensely focussed on his mission. Was he harmless, or did he regard postmen as litter? "What do you do with the litter?"

"I dump it." Al nodded vigorously. "I collect it in my car first, then when the car is full, I dump it. Look, I'll show you."

He led me over to the station wagon. Now that I was closer to it, I could see the source of the stench. Al had piled rubbish of all kinds high on the back seat of the car: plastic containers, beer bottles, soft drink cans, ice cream sticks, rotting fruit, sodden newspapers, chocolate wrappers, the detritus of modern society's commercial products. Amongst it all, shadowy shapes darted.

I turned, about to be sick, and stopped myself only because Al stood right in my path.

"These are my treasures." He took a handful of metal objects from his pocket. "Found them two nights ago. Haven't found these before."

I forced myself to look at what he held in his open hand, afraid it would be something revolting.

It was four spent 12-gauge shotgun cartridges.

"Al, this is important: tell me exactly where and when you got those."

Chapter 20

FROM THE MODERATE warmth and comparative fresh air of my car, I called the inspector.

"O'Toole here."

"Inspector, do you have an ID on that latest victim yet?"

"Not yet, Ashcroft. I'll let you know when we do. But we do have an approximate time of death. About thirty-six to forty-eight hours ago."

"Okay, good to know. I've got some information for you, too. I know where the crime scene is." I gave the location of a property outside the western fringe of the city, a little west of Tornby.

"How did you come about that information?"

"Pure chance. I've been interviewing people with a history of mental illness and violence. That included Al Phillips today. He's crazy, but probably harmless. He found some 12-gauge shotgun cartridges outside this address while out cleaning up litter."

"Text me his details. I'll send someone to bring him in. Fancy him for these murders, do you?"

"No. He's eccentric—I mean, he has delusions—but I don't think he's dangerous."

"So, he has delusions, and you found him with spent shotgun cartridges. Sounds like a prime suspect to me. We'll interview him."

"All right." Al Phillips was possibly unstable and unpredictable. Who knew what he might do?

"You said he had violence in his background."

"Punched his mother's abusive partner as a teenager. In my book, that should have earned him a medal, not detention. I can't imagine him as a serial killer."

"We'll see. I'll go to that address you gave me, see what I can find there."

"I'll meet you there." I disconnected, called Deepa and updated her, then headed over to the property where Al Phillips had found the shotgun cartridges.

I was the first to arrive. This was an area of lifestyle blocks, where houses were further apart and owners liked to raise chickens, ride horses and drive ride-on lawnmowers. There could even be owls out here.

A long gravel driveway led to a modern house with a shiny silver Toyota Yaris parked outside. Chickens ran about in the yard. Tall trees that served as a windbreak swayed in the breeze. Numerous other trees of all kinds dotted the expansive front lawn.

Al Phillips had told me he'd found the shotgun cartridges on the pavement. I sensed something had happened here. Whether it was something I'd unconsciously seen, or smelled, I wasn't sure. Who knows, maybe the owls had started talking to me.

Then I saw it: the newish-looking Yaris had a smashed wing mirror. Not only smashed, but obliterated. Little of it remained attached to the car—most of it was scattered on the ground.

I walked up to the front door and knocked. No answer.

I poked around some more and discovered a hole in the side of the house. It looked like a shotgun slug could have made it.

O'Toole and Amy Ling arrived, and I pointed it out to them. Amy called headquarters for a police photographer and SOCOs.

We'd found the crime scene, all right.

Deepa turned up and parked her scooter at the gate.

Amy got off the phone. "This is the address of a Chris Dodd. No one's reported him missing, but his photo ID looks like the body." She blushed. "I mean—"

"Yeah, passport photos are terrible, but I know what you mean. He's our unknown dead victim." Poor guy.

"Yes."

"Find out what you can about him, Amy." The inspector turned to me, but I was already looking for a way inside. His words followed me as I approached the front porch. "Ashford, this was a good lead, but you should leave the scene to the SOCOs."

I pretended not to hear him and unlocked the front door using the hole I'd just made by smashing a stone through a glass pane. Someone could be inside, injured. Deepa followed me into the house, camera poised.

It was dark and cold as if someone had turned the heating off a few days ago.

I stopped in the hallway by the open door into the living room. It was a mess in there. Shattered glass lay on the floor. Someone had slashed sofas, criss-cross, with a blade. Books lay in haphazard piles at the foot of partly emptied bookcases. A television had a wooden stool sticking out from the screen.

It was as if a major earthquake had hit—but we hadn't had one big enough to cause that amount of damage for years.

I kept looking. Something didn't seem right. After a few moments, I worked out what it was—there were no family photos anywhere.

Deepa shouted from the next room. "In here." I joined her, O'Toole and Amy in the kitchen.

If anything, the kitchen was worse. Broken plates and bowls and glasses peppered the floor, crunching underneath my shoes like cornflakes. A table lay on its side.

Deepa had paled. Amy, her mouth turned down, looked at something behind the table, out of my line of sight.

O'Toole reached out and grabbed my arm to prevent me from going further. "We don't want to contaminate the scene any more than we already have."

Chapter 21

BLOOD. Pooled, dried blood. Presumably Dodd's. The perp had killed him here, in his own home.

Deepa turned away from the grisly scene and went into an adjacent room. "Back door's open." The pitch of her voice rose almost to breaking point. "Oh, the dog… the poor dog. What sicko would do that?"

I went to her, then outside through the open doorway. A golden Labrador lay on the back lawn, dead, shot in the torso. Contained by a fenced dog run, it couldn't have been any threat to the murderer.

Nausea roiled in my stomach. Why kill the dog when it was secured? It had to be significant somehow. But how?

O'Toole came up behind me. "When did your guy say he picked up those cartridges? And where from, exactly?"

"Two nights ago, about eight o'clock. He said they were on the pavement in front of the driveway."

Amy appeared at the doorway, next to Deepa. "You will want to hear this. Chris Dodd worked for NZ Post, same as Ricky Cohen."

O'Toole smiled grimly. "There's a connection at last. But why are postal workers the target?"

"Not only postal workers. It doesn't link up with the dead pensioner, Gary Smith. It could be a coincidence." Though I didn't believe in coincidences like this one.

"True." O'Toole frowned.

"And the M.O.'s different. Ricky Cohen and Gary Smith were murdered on the street in daylight. Chris Dodd was murdered at home and his body dumped elsewhere."

The inspector tapped the side of his head, as if indicating he'd just had a remarkable idea. "Maybe it's a different serial killer. Serial killers always have the same M.O."

I groaned inwardly.

Deepa turned away. "I'm leaving. I've got a deadline to make and a lot to write about. And I can't bear to look at that poor dog." She disappeared back the way we had come.

I'd seen enough too and went outside. The first of the SOCOs were arriving.

I found Deepa sitting astride her Vespa, strapping on her helmet, and hurried over before she took off. "I'm going to the NZ Post depot. I want to speak to Dave about Chris Dodd before the office shuts for the day. I'll call you afterwards."

"You'll have to hurry. I think they close soon."

I drove as fast as legally permitted plus ten kilometres an hour, enough to earn me a fine if a sharp traffic cop pulled me over. Thankfully, all the speed cameras in the city had suffered the same fate as the traffic cameras. A lot of stuff didn't work anymore since the quakes, and the people in charge had either left town or always had more important things to worry about.

I reached the NZ Post depot three minutes before they were due to close for the day and parked. The receptionist and I raced each other to the door, but I managed to squeeze in before she could shut it and turn the sign to 'Closed'.

"Is Dave still here?"

"If you're lucky." The receptionist frowned and returned to her desk. I guess she didn't want to stay late, but she phoned his office and spoke to him.

He came out carrying a bulky sports bag. I tried to guess the contents. Squash racket? Football gear? Change of clothes? Or a shotgun? He wouldn't be the first manager to downsize his team by shooting them.

Dave's forehead creased when he saw me. "What are you doing here?" He took a deep breath. "Is there any news?"

"Sorry, this isn't about Ricky Cohen. It's about another employee of yours, Chris Dodd."

"I haven't seen Chris for two days. It's his days off. I tried calling him to see if he'd do some extra shifts, take over for Ricky. He didn't answer."

So, this was the guy Dave mentioned last time, as I suspected. "He's dead."

Dave dropped his bag. It clunked to the floor. He staggered back a step. The receptionist, being closer to him, took his arm and directed him to a chair in the waiting area. "I'll get some water." She hurried off, looking pale.

"What happened?" Dave groaned and didn't meet my eyes.

His reaction intrigued me, and I studied him. Was it a deliberate exaggeration, an act, or was he genuinely distraught about the untimely deaths of his employees?

"We don't know much yet." I didn't want to reveal any details. Inspector O'Toole would be furious if I primed Dave with the facts before a constable could question him.

I took a seat near Dave. The receptionist returned with three cups of water and shared them around. It was cool and refreshing. Just what I needed. And it gave Dave a little time to stew.

"Can you at least tell me how he died?" Dave's breathing rasped.

"Murdered."

"Oh god! What's wrong with the world?" It came out as a high-pitched wail, taking me by surprise.

The receptionist spoke up. "The *Richter Mail* says there's a serial killer on the loose, striking at random. I'm almost too afraid to go out."

"Newspapers exaggerate so they sell more copies." Though it was her job, Deepa was stirring up fear on the page.

"At least the city's most brilliant private detective is on the case."

I lowered my gaze demurely, but before I could say anything, the receptionist, now quite talkative, continued. "Have you met him, this brilliant detective, in your investigations?"

I clamped my jaw shut.

"Never mind me." Maybe she sensed that I would not answer. "I'll be off now, if you don't need me." Dave said nothing, so the receptionist grabbed her handbag and left.

I turned to Dave. His breathing had become more normal. "Can you think of any reason why someone would want to kill Chris Dodd?"

"Not at all. He's never been in any trouble that I know of. Friendly, polite, professional at all times. Married, no children. An ordinary guy."

If he's married, where's his wife? Why hasn't she missed him for the past two days? "You said earlier that you tried to call Chris to take over from Ricky after Ricky's murder. So, he was a reliable guy?"

"Yes, but not just that. Chris and Ricky used to swap postal routes once a month. In fact, they'd just swapped on the day Ricky was shot."

I froze for a moment while I took this in. "You mean the day Ricky was shot, it was his first day back on the route Chris had been working on for a month?"

"Yes, exactly. Is that important?"

I didn't answer. It might be vital. It might be nothing. It was one of those coincidences I didn't like.

"You've been very helpful, Dave, thanks, but before you go home, I've got one last question: Did you know a man called Gary Smith, retired, late sixties?"

Dave shook his head.

"Okay, thanks."

I bid him goodbye and returned to my car, which I'd movie-parked right in front of the building.

It was dusk. The shadows in the interior of my car concealed my presence.

O'Toole needed to know that the two dead men shared the same postal route. If I wanted access to the next crime scenes—I shuddered at the thought that there might be more of them—I needed to share my information like I'd promised.

My phone was in my hand, but I couldn't make the call. Why not?

I wanted to solve the case on my own, prove to myself, Deepa, O'Toole and even my dead parents that I was what I claimed: a capable private investigator. Being unable to solve my parents' murders had always nagged at my self-confidence. I'd learned everything I could about criminology and forensic psychology. I could find this killer, I knew it.

But there was no place for selfishness and withholding information from the police with a murderer on the loose. The more people hunting the perp, the better.

Several cars approached from the car park behind the Post depot. Workers leaving. Security lights illuminated them as they passed the front entrance and made their way past me to the road. SUVs, hatchbacks, and one dark station wagon.

I sat bolt upright, peering through the gloom. In the pool of murky light, I had the briefest glimpse of the driver. It looked like Dave, but I couldn't be sure.

Should I follow him?

I reached for the ignition key, and my phone rang.

It was O'Toole. I answered it.

He snapped at me. "Where are you?"

"At the NZ Post depot. I told the manager that Chris Dodd is dead."

"You did what? You've primed him before we can interview him ourselves."

"I didn't reveal any details, Inspector, just told him about the death. He might have found out about that through the media anyway before your officers question him."

"All right. How did he take it?"

"He was… expressive."

"Meaning?"

"He either truly cares for his staff, or he could audition for Hamlet."

"Got it. Thanks, Ashford. Listen, Dodd's married, but his wife's in Australia for a few days. We've broken the grave news to her. She'll be flying back tomorrow."

I also called Deepa to update her, but we didn't talk for long. She was writing her article, and my update meant she had to start again. As for me, I needed time to collect my thoughts and piece the evidence together.

Time could be running out for the next victim.

Chapter 22

Day 4, evening

I STOPPED AT Quake Burgers on the way home for dinner and ate at a table in the corner, my fedora pulled down low so no one would recognise me. I often preferred to eat alone and in peace so I could think.

At about seven thirty, I got home, only to discover the door to my apartment was unlocked. My breath caught. I edged inside, wary, ready for anything. But I needn't have worried. It was only Deepa. She was lying on the sofa in my living room with Torquemada curled up on her stomach.

"How did you get in?"

"Your neighbour let me in with the spare key. She gave me a sly look too, like she thought you and I were getting it on." Deepa's gaze bore into me.

"Really?" I coughed. My cheeks warmed. "Did you get your article written?"

"Yep, and it's a damn good one. My editor, Don Bailey, told me it was time to step it up, make it—"

"More sensational?" I slung my raincoat and fedora onto a chair, too tired to hang them up.

"I suppose so. I'm still reporting the truth, Danny, I'm simply dressing it up a bit."

"That's what you call it, is it?" I might pretend that her articles were too sensational, not serious enough to warrant reading, but I read them anyway over a breakfast pastry. "So, you want a juicier psychological profile for the killer? Wilder theories about the motive?"

"What I do isn't easy, you know." She glared at me. "I'm competing with staff reporters. I have to dig deeper, find fresh material, organise it, interpret it, ask penetrating questions and draw conclusions. I have to write to a tight word count and a looming deadline. And it's got to be something that pulls in readers and engages them."

"You're right. Sorry, Deepa, let's not argue. It's been a hard day, and I'm trying to make sense of it all."

Her voice softened. "Let's discuss the case after dinner, Danny. That's why I'm here. Everything's moving so fast with the case, we need to use every spare minute."

"I agree."

"Have you eaten?"

"No." I didn't want to pass up the chance of sharing a meal with her, so I lied.

"I hope you like Indian. I brought the ingredients for chicken jalfrezi with me."

"Sounds perfect." Whatever that was.

"You can cook next time."

Ah. Cooking. There's a reason I eat so many takeaways. I mainly used the kitchen to make coffees and to store cat food.

I lifted Torquemada off Deepa and put him in his basket. She swung her legs over the edge of the sofa and stood up.

"How do you have your curry? Indian hot or English hot?"

"Mild."

"All right. Live dangerously." She grinned and went into the kitchen.

I followed. "Can I help?" Please say 'no'.

"No need. It's a simple meal."

She poured some rice into a round thing, added boiling water and switched it on. A few minutes later, she'd put meat and vegetables into a pot, added a jar of sauce, and put it on the hob.

"Now I've done that, we can talk for a while. Do you have any wine?"

I poured her a red, and a shot of whiskey for myself. We took our drinks into the living room. I sat on the sofa, and she plonked down next to me.

"I've come up with a moniker for the killer: 'The Messenger Shooter.'"

I sipped my drink. "Must you glorify the perp?"

"It's communication, not glorification. The public like a catchy name."

I frowned. "It's hardly in the same league as 'The Boston Strangler' or 'Jack the Ripper.'"

"That's the best I could come up with five minutes before the deadline. The crucial thing is that it'll fix in the public's mind. He'll become more real to them now."

"I see." Was that a good thing?

She looked to the floor. "Seeing that dead dog was too much. It wasn't any threat to the killer, who shot it anyway. So cold-blooded. That affected me even more than that poor dead man in the Red Zone. I don't know why."

"Accumulated stress, I'd say."

"Do you ever get used to it?"

"No…" I paused to consider what to say next. "But it does get easier. I tell myself my job is to look for clues, study the scene and figure out what happened and in what order. I need to be dispassionate to be effective."

"So, that makes it less difficult pretending to yourself that the horror doesn't affect you?"

"Something like that, yes, and it allows me to do my job."

"Right." Her voice wavered. "Do you think Inspector O'Toole is capable of solving this case?"

"O'Toole's a decent guy at heart, even if he's arrogant and overconfident. But, to answer your question, no, I don't think he can solve this, not without a lucky break. It's too complicated. There's nothing much to go on. The killer is unpredictable. And, following the earthquakes, with Quake City being left to fend for itself, the police force is nowhere near as good as it was before. There's no money for resources. The cops here are the lowest paid in the country, so anyone who's any good left a long time ago."

Deepa nodded. Her eyes shone like pools of intelligent darkness, deep, mysterious, and captivating. Almost too enchanting for me.

"Can you solve it, Danny?"

"I have to, Deepa." I bit my cheek. Had I made a promise I couldn't keep?

"I've been thinking about the postmen. It might simply be a coincidence that they were working the same route."

"Yeah, I wondered that too. Ricky Cohen was shot while delivering the mail. Chris Dodd was killed at home. Different circumstances. And Gary Smith was a pensioner, not a postie. And Liz Nicholls is a courier driver."

"Gary Smith was delivering advertisements to mailboxes, though." Deepa shrugged. "Everyone was involved in delivering messages of some kind. That's why I came up with 'The Messenger Shooter.'"

"You don't say? I'd never have worked that out if you hadn't told me."

She shot me a sharp glance, then smiled when she recognised my sarcasm.

"I agree with you." I spoke slowly, still deliberating the idea in my mind. "The killer has some vendetta against people delivering packages, letters, advertisements. Maybe there's some past trauma involved and some recent event has triggered it."

"Or the killer's a sicko, hearing voices telling him to do awful things."

"Yes, could be. That's why I wanted to question people with a history of mental illness and violence. The trouble is there's too many of them."

"Even more since the earthquakes." Deepa shuddered. Perhaps she had some personal trauma herself. I hadn't asked.

"There's a lot of people in Quake City with mental illness to some degree, but only a small percentage are violent."

"How about this for an idea? Both postmen worked the same route. Maybe the killer targeted them deliberately because they were involved in something on that route. Drug dealing, maybe."

"Possible, but if that were the case, how would it link to Gary Smith and Liz Nicholls?"

Deepa wobbled her head from side to side. "It's just a thought. I don't know."

"Yeah, I don't know either. But I don't like coincidences. In my business, what looks like a coincidence usually turns out to be otherwise."

The stovetop timer dinged. "Dinner time. Give me five minutes." Deepa stood and went into the kitchen.

I don't have a dining table—no room or inclination—so I cleared some space on the coffee table.

Deepa brought out the food in bowls. It smelled tantalising. Despite having eaten an hour ago, my mouth watered.

"This is better than burgers, isn't it?" She set the bowls down.

"Sure smells like it. Thank you." I ate a spoonful. My taste buds exploded with delight, and then with fire. "I thought you said this would be mild."

"Oh. I forgot. It's not too spicy, is it?"

"It's delicious." My throat burned like an inferno.

"If it's too spicy, drink a glass of milk. That will help."

"Okay, thanks." My voice was a croak.

I fetched the milk. It quelled some of the burning sensation. The meal was tasty; I simply wasn't used to the spiciness of it.

Deepa finished eating first and watched me. "Do you ever listen to the talk-show radio? Alice Hadwin is doing a special call-in on the murders tonight. I think we should listen."

I swallowed. "I've never heard of her. Yes, let's listen. If she's taking callers, maybe we'll learn something."

I washed our dinner things, made some coffee, then we talked more until it was time for the talk show. Deepa activated an app on her phone—a device that had more uses than I could ever have imagined—and the radio personality's voice projected forth.

Chapter 23

"GOOD EVENING, Quake City. Tonight, we're tackling the subject of the latest string of murders. They've all taken place in the southern suburbs." Her voice was edgy, strident, confident—and it compelled listening. "Residents, lock your doors! Keep off the streets! There's a psycho with a shotgun on the loose in the leafy suburbs by the hills."

"And you accused me of being sensationalist? Catch her tone?" Deepa tilted her head, her eyebrow raised.

An uncomfortable feeling tickled my stomach, like spiders crawling over bare skin. What was Hadwin's angle here? Boosting her show's ratings by scaring the public?

"Let's sum up the situation, listeners. The first murder was three days ago: a postman killed on his rounds with a single shot. Yesterday, a pensioner shot dead while out walking. And today, the third victim: another postman, murdered in the Red Zone—or should we call that the Dead Zone, listeners?"

"She's not thorough with her fact-checking." Deepa sipped her coffee.

"You mean she's wildly inaccurate. Chris Dodd wasn't murdered in the Red Zone, and he was the second victim, not the third. He was murdered no later than two nights ago."

"It's not the content of the message that's important to her and her listeners. It's the way she gets the message across. She riles people up."

"Yeah, I'm getting that."

Alice Hadwin didn't pause. She ploughed on, berating the police, the council, the government (even though they had little to do with Quake City ever since they cut it loose after the earthquakes), the younger generation, the older generation, the generation in-between. Everyone was at fault, and in combination created a breeding ground for serial killers. Or so she claimed.

"Three murders in four days! When will it stop, listeners? Will there be a murder tomorrow, or will the killer take a break? My advice to you, listeners, is this: keep looking behind you. And now we'll take some calls. Paula is on line one. What do you have to say, Paula?"

"Someone has to stop this madman, Alice."

"Sure, Paula, but not too soon. This is the most exciting thing that's happened in Quake City for ages." Canned laughter. Paula started to protest before Alice cut her off mid-word. "Sorry, we seem to have lost Paula there. Oh, that was a joke, everyone. I'll take this seriously now. We have a serial killer out there. An angry person. Maybe a sick person. Someone who hates people. Maybe people hate him? If only we could look into his life through a crystal ball and see the colour of his heart. Was he born evil, or has society turned him evil?"

"I can't believe that woman." I shook my head. "She's making this whole situation seem like a story or reality TV. Unreal. Who listens to this crap?"

"Well, we are." Deepa's voice was quiet, hesitant.

"For professional reasons only, Deepa."

"I admit, she's a callous bitch, but I think that's why many people like her. She appeals to people's base emotions, says things out loud that they might not admit to thinking themselves."

Deepa had a point.

The next caller was on. Duncan from Crapanui. "I'm terrified to go out of my house. How am I supposed to buy my beer and ciggies?"

"Who cares? You're safe in the northern suburbs. The killer's working the exclusive southern suburbs." She said the last three words with an affected, snooty voice. "Get over it. Right, Duncan's gone. Any new callers? Jenny's on line four. What are your thoughts, Jenny?"

"I'm scared, Alice. Too scared to leave the house. And I live in the south, not like your last caller. In Crackcroft."

"I think you're safe, Jenny. All the victims have been men."

"That's good to hear. Oh, I feel so much better now."

"But who knows what goes on in the mind of a psycho killer? He might attack a woman next, so stay indoors, Jenny. Good night. Any more callers? None yet. Let's have some words from our sponsors."

My eyes widened at her attitude, and I ran my hand through my hair. "Why did you want to listen to this? She's almost as crazy as the killer."

"Like you said. Professional interest. I don't like it, I certainly don't like her, but it's relevant to what we're working on. Some of her listeners are my readers. I need to know how she's directing the mob."

Directing the mob. I nodded. That sounded about right.

"Quake City, let's get back to the discussion. Was there another murder during the commercial break? No? Of course not. Postmen don't work in the evening. Not like me! Ha ha."

"I don't think I can take much more of this." I had my head in my hands.

Deepa grimaced. Maybe she felt the same.

"We have another caller. No name given. Okay, an anonymous caller. What's on your mind, caller-with-no-name?"

"Shut up."

That silenced even Alice for a few moments, but only a few. Then she was back in her stride. "I sense resentment. Fury, even. Tell me what's going on, caller-with-no-name."

"Stop talking about me."

Three seconds of pure silence. I stopped breathing. My heart missed a beat. Deepa's eyes opened wide.

Alice started up again. "I don't take crank callers on this show, no-name-girl. Explain yourself in five seconds or I'll cut you off."

Keep them on the line, I screamed in my head. A moment later, Alice's words hit me. A girl? Could our perp be female? It wasn't the usual profile, but nothing was normal in this case.

In the background of the call, music from the Quake City Rockers started up. The caller spoke. "I got him, I did, for what he did to—"

"Get lost, asshole." A click sounded as Alice disconnected them. "Any legitimate callers? Anyone scared? Anyone with a story? No? Time for another commercial break."

"Was that actually the killer?" Deepa's eyes opened wide as plates.

"Impossible to know. Maybe." I stared at her phone as if it held secrets to reveal.

"I couldn't tell if it was a man with an unusual voice or a woman with a low voice. And that cow cut them off when they were about to divulge something."

"I'll call O'Toole. He can get the phone records. We'll find out where the call came from first thing tomorrow."

"Never mind that. I have a contact who can do that for us in minutes. My hacker friend. I'll call her."

Deepa was resourceful. When had I gone from thinking of her as a liability to my investigation, to considering her as an asset?

She made the call. I gathered that the contact was a schoolgirl with a nifty talent and an inclination for hacking into government departments, businesses, schools, wherever she wanted. All illegal, but useful. I should get her business card, or whatever it is teenage hackers have.

"Thanks, Petra." Deepa disconnected. "She was studying for an exam, but she went in for me. That last call to Alice came from a pay-as-you-go phone near the Riverside shops."

I stood. "Let's go. They might still be there."

Chapter 24

I GRABBED MY RAINCOAT and hat and was at the door in moments.

"Even if that's the case, how would we know? We've got no idea what they look like, only a vague description of a dark station wagon, or a vehicle like one. And we couldn't work out if the caller was male or female."

"Never mind. Are you coming?"

"Yep." She left her laptop on the coffee table, grabbed her bag and purple puffer jacket, and joined me.

We hurried downstairs to the car and got in. At this time in the late evening, the traffic was thin. It took two minutes to get there, as the Riverside shops were around the corner from my apartment. Most were dark, closed up for the night. A fitness centre was still open. And the Coffee and Cheesequake never closed.

It was about nine thirty. People wandered the streets, going to and from the gym and the café. I didn't judge our killer to be a fitness fanatic, so we went to the carpark by the café.

We scanned the cars in the semi-darkness, looking for anything matching the vague description the witnesses had given us. But it was futile. Coming out here on the spur of the moment with nothing definite to look for was grasping at hypotheticals, a measure of how desperate I was to have a breakthrough in this case. So desperate that I'd hoped Fate would look upon me with kindness for a moment. No such luck. Fate's a bitch.

"We're wasting our time." I hit the steering wheel with my palm. "The caller could've been anywhere around here and has probably long gone."

"They might have got a coffee after making the call and still be here somewhere."

"What's the chance of that?" Frustration crept into my voice.

"Better than zero. I know from my experience as a reporter you have to take every chance there is, no matter how small. Maybe one in twenty work out. This could be the one. Let's keep looking."

"I guess you're right." I swerved into the carpark area itself. Three station wagons, all dark colours, sat next to each other along the edge by the roadside.

"Triple strike." Deepa punched the air.

"Three out of the thousands of cars like this in Quake City."

I pulled into an empty park two spaces further along. We got out and walked back to the station wagons, peering through the windows. Would the killer be so careless as to leave a shotgun lying on the back seat? Or covered up by something like a blanket? Unlikely.

The first car had baby seats. I doubted that was our perp.

Deepa moved past me to check out the second car. "Family car here. School gear in the back."

We were about to move on to the third car together when something caught my eye, and my ear. A navy-blue station wagon turning out of the carpark, with the Quake City Rockers' discordant music filling the air. In the dark, I couldn't get a clear view of the driver.

"Hurry." I was already running. "We need to follow that car."

Deepa followed my line of vision, then hurried after me. She scrambled inside as I started the car. "Don't let it out of your sight."

I reversed out of the car park and drove over the kerbing separating the parking spaces from the exit. The car jolted and crunched like an avalanche of bones, but made it. I swerved onto the road, forcing a car to brake, the screeches hitting my eardrums as darts.

"Don't get us killed, please. I have deadlines to meet."

Deadlines? Was she joking? "Where did the car go?"

"Take the next left."

The traffic light was red, but the way was clear, so I ploughed through.

Deepa clenched her jaw. "It must be the perp. I think they know we're onto them. That manoeuvre of yours wasn't subtle. They went through the same red light before us."

"I didn't have time to go around the carpark. We'd definitely have lost them."

"Go faster. They're getting away."

I put my foot to the floor, and the Swift sped up. Ahead, the taillights of the station wagon came on as it screeched around a corner onto a road by the river.

I reached the same corner, slowed for the turn, then raced in pursuit. The road curved, and for a few seconds I lost sight of the vehicle before it reappeared not as far in front as before.

A loud crack pierced the night, then another. The station wagon passed under a street light. It veered as the driver leaned out, shooting at us. Even in the dim glow from the streetlight, I couldn't determine if the driver was a man or a woman.

Deepa cried out. "Shit! Pull over."

For a moment, I wasn't going to do that. The killer, possibly panicking, shooting from a moving car at a moving target, and whom I believed to be a poor shot in any case, wasn't likely to hit us.

But the bullets were going somewhere. Maybe into the neighbouring houses.

I stopped the car. Regret swept over me. I didn't want to let the perp get away, but I couldn't give them more opportunity to fire erratically in our direction and put Deepa at risk.

One last shot shattered the driver's side headlight of my Swift.

"Hell's teeth. He's hit the car." I watched the taillights of the station wagon disappear around another bend.

"He could've killed us." Deepa's voice was trill. She reached for me.

I gave her a hug. She shivered in my arms.

"We're okay. That was a lucky shot." An unlucky one for the Swift.

She calmed down. "Do you often get shot at?"

"From time to time. Fortunately, most people are lousy shots. I'm going to call O'Toole."

I made the call, though I already knew it was too late. The killer had spotted us tailing them from the beginning, and must have driven into the warren of streets by the river to lose us.

"No, I didn't get the plate number. It all happened too fast." And once I'd got behind the perp's car, it was too far away to read it.

The inspector said he would send out patrol cars, but I'd lost hope. The perp had eluded us this time. Damnation! Would they kill again before they were caught, because I'd let them get away? I cringed.

I turned the car around and headed back the way we'd come. Our time hadn't been wasted—we'd confirmed the killer's vehicle was a navy-blue station wagon.

The engine of the Swift sounded different somehow. Rougher. Maybe it needed a service. Or maybe the slug had done more damage than smashing the headlight.

Deepa sighed. "Where are we going?"

"To the Coffee and Cheesequake."

"Wonderful idea. I need a coffee and a cakeaway after that."

"Not just that. I want to ask them if they remember the driver of that car. Maybe someone even knows who they are."

No such luck. The staff were no help at all. The only people they recognised—their regulars—were still in the café.

We'd had the killer in our sights, and they'd slipped away. Would the chance come again?

Disheartened, I drove us back to my apartment and parked in front. Rain started pattering on the footpath as we stepped out of the car.

Deepa's laptop was on the coffee table, so she came in to get it.

I threw my keys onto the desk, hung up my coat and hat, then followed Deepa into the living room. She sat on the sofa, head in hands, shaking her head from side to side.

"Deepa, what's going on?"

She gave a strangled sob. "He could have killed us. What the hell am I doing writing about this psycho? He—she—I don't know, the perp shot at us."

I sat and took one of her hands away from her face and held it in my own.

"You're fine. You've had a shock, but you're okay. The killer doesn't know who you are or where you are. You're safe."

She nodded slowly. "The police aren't going to catch them, are they? Not without a lot of luck."

"The killer will make a mistake at some point. And we'll keep digging and interviewing people. Sooner or later, we'll find them or come across someone who knows who they are. The perp can't hide forever."

"I don't know. It's too dangerous, Danny. Maybe we should give up. You'll get your cut of the money I've earned from writing articles. You don't have to go on and put yourself in danger to solve these murders."

"I can't stop. I'm stubborn that way."

"I thought you might say that."

"You're getting to know me. Try not to worry. I'll track them down, and you'll get the scoop of the year."

"As long as it isn't your obituary."

"If it is, make sure it's your best work, okay?"

Deepa punched me on the arm. "Danny, I'm being serious. I'm frightened."

I set my jaw. "I've got to catch this killer. They'll keep killing until someone stops them. I can't drop it now. I need to keep going."

Deepa stared at me with those deep, brown, beautiful eyes of hers for what seemed like ages. Finally, she agreed. "All right. I had a shock, that's all, but I'm okay. I brought you into this, so we'll finish it together. Partners." She raised her fist for a fist pump. I obliged.

"Let's start again tomorrow after you've had some rest and a chance to recover. We can interview more people from our lists, dig deeper into the history of the victims so far, liaise with the police. Something might turn up. We have to get lucky sometime."

"Sounds good."

I glanced at my watch. Ten thirty.

"Danny, can I stay here tonight? I'm just… um… still a bit nervous."

The way I looked at her must have conveyed something, or maybe she imagined it, for she clarified: "Not like that. It's late. We'll want to make an early start. I'll sleep on the sofa."

I sighed, trying not to let my thoughts run away with me. What had she seen in my eyes?

"Torquemada sleeps on the sofa. He'll probably end up sleeping on your face. You take the bed. I'll sleep on the sofa."

"If you're sure…"

"Yes. I often get up and work or drink alone at my desk because I can't sleep." And I don't have any friends to drink with. "It makes sense for you to take the bedroom where's there's more privacy."

"Okay. Thanks. I appreciate it, Danny."

I nodded. My stomach fluttered and my breathing was heavy. As I expected, I didn't sleep well.

Chapter 25

Day 4, night

CAN'T SLEEP. Something's wrong. I'm sure he took the car out again tonight—it's parked in a different place now—but I don't know what for or what he did.

His clothes are on the bathroom floor again. At least they're not bloody this time.

There's no one I can talk to about this. No one. I don't want to go back to that place where the whitecoats kept me.

I'll just keep quiet.

Maybe he'll go away.

Chapter 26

Day 5, morning

WE HAD BREAKFAST at the Coffee and Cheesequake café after buying a copy of the *Richter Mail*. Deepa opened it and searched for her article.

"Page four! I expected page three at least." She crumpled the paper and took a sharp intake of breath. "The copy editor butchered it. I toiled over this piece—"

"I thought you rewrote most of it in half an hour." I took a bite of an almond pastry.

"Yep, that's true, but she's chopped it all around and messed it up completely! That's not what I wrote."

"Let me have a look." I turned the newspaper toward me and read the article. "Maybe it's a bit sensationalist, but the information's there."

"You think it's all right?"

"Yes, it's good."

"Actually, I think she only changed a few words. And all the best stuff is mine."

I chuckled. I'd uncovered a tender spot for Deepa: other people's opinions of her writing. I imagined her in constant battles with copy editors and their red pens. Truly mightier than the sword.

She folded the newspaper and stuffed it into her backpack. "What's your plan for after breakfast?"

"How about we interview some more people on our shortlist?"

She shook her head. "It might work, but it's a long shot. A few people with a mental health issue in the past who just happen to own a station wagon."

I nodded. That had been my angle of investigation. "And who'd been violent. What's the problem?"

"It's too narrow. What if the killer lives outside the area we limited the data search to? What if they've never been hospitalised, or even diagnosed? What if they're on the list and we interview them—all that will do is tip them off that we might be onto them, won't it?"

She had valid points. "It's an approach that relies on a lot of luck, yes… the key is finding a likely suspect who we can link to the crimes, yet make them think we're not interested in them until we find evidence."

Deepa took a swig of her cooled coffee. "It's leaving too much to chance. We came up with that list when we had absolutely nothing to go on, merely as a starting point to give us something—anything—to do. Now that we know more, there should be a better use of our time."

"What do you suggest?" It wasn't easy to keep the annoyance out of my voice. Deepa wasn't the private investigator here—I was. But she was my client, or partner, now. I should at least listen to her idea. I took a large bite out of my almond croissant to cover up any disagreeable expression I might have had. It's hard to appear grumpy with a mouthful of French pastry.

"The perp has killed three people, apparently for no reason. Surely even crazy killers don't shoot people at random. Do they?"

"Unfortunately, some of them do. Some of them are purely evil; others act because they are extremely unwell and can't block out voices in their head telling them to kill."

"But there must be a reason? What's the point in a life that's snuffed out purely by chance, on the whim of a madman?"

I sat back in my chair. There was something more going on here for Deepa than I'd understood at first. "What are you really worried about, Deepa?"

"The killer could target anyone. Me. You. Literally anyone, for no reason. That's what's so scary."

"The unpredictability of it. I agree that's frightening. But, although we can't find any reason why the killer picked those victims specifically, there is a pattern. Two were postmen, the other was delivering pamphlets. The perp's not just targeting anyone. Also, he or she threatened that courier driver, Liz Nicholls, but didn't shoot. Maybe they're only targeting men."

Deepa's worry lines faded a little. "I don't understand why they're doing it. This pattern, I mean. And why kill the dog?"

"I don't know, but I think the dog is significant somehow." I considered this for a few seconds and, in that time, signalled the waitress and asked for another coffee each for Deepa and I. She had cleared the table already. We needed to order again or move on.

"Maybe something happened to the killer years ago. Or something related to that area of town. Perhaps a postman was… you know, knocking twice. Having an affair with his mother while his father was at work. Or with the father while the mother was at work. Who knows?"

Deepa laughed. "You've been reading too many novels."

"No, it's possible. The perp might have harboured a grudge against postmen for years, and then there was some trigger that sent them postal." I winced at my inadvertent pun.

"That's not even remotely funny."

"I didn't mean it to be. There's another possibility too. Remember me mentioning voices in the head of the killer? Maybe that's it. Have you heard of the phrase 'Don't shoot the messenger'?"

She nodded.

"Perhaps that's twisted around in the killer's mind so he or she thinks they have to 'shoot the messenger'. Perhaps they're fixated on that idea and can't stop themselves."

"I get it. And if they were obsessed with the phrase 'Too many cooks spoil the broth', they might be out killing chefs because that's what the voices tell them to do."

"Exactly."

"So, which is it, do you think?" Deepa twirled a strand of her hair, musing. "Voices in the head? Or a past trauma brought back to mind—and what could the trigger event have been? Or could it even be both?"

I shook my head. "I don't know yet. If it's a reaction to a past trauma being triggered, that will at least give us a chance to find out what it is and identify the killer. If they're driven by voices in the head, then it could be anyone, and it might take us longer to find them."

"So, let's concentrate on the first option. Maybe something happened that affected the killer when he or she was younger that connects them with one of the victims. Then something recently set them off on a murderous rampage. We can check through the news archive."

"Great idea." I tried to keep the lack of enthusiasm out of my voice. Scanning microfiches and old newspapers would be torture.

Chapter 27

Day 5, afternoon

FIVE HOURS OF SOME of the most tedious investigation work I've ever done passed in what seemed like a century. I walked up and down the aisles, I pinched myself, I drank a lot of coffee to stay awake. Reading old news was boring, yet Deepa enjoyed it and would often speak up about some irrelevant and long-forgotten titbit of news that she found interesting.

I was about to say she could continue to work this angle on her own while I went to interrogate more people from my shortlist, when her phone buzzed. Mixed feelings flooded through me. It was a relief from this monotony, but it might signify another murder or murder attempt.

Deepa read the message, then passed the phone to me. She trembled and slumped to the floor against the wall.

I grimaced. It was another death, all right. A different area, though: Parkside, north of the southern suburbs where the earlier murders had taken place.

Had the killer changed their pattern? Or was there no pattern at all?

"Are you okay?" I crouched down next to her.

"Yep. It's just… like a ticking time bomb. This is the fourth murder in five days. Will it ever stop?"

"No." I shook my head grimly. "Now the perp's gone this far, they won't stop, probably *can't* stop, even if they want to."

"What are we going to do, Danny? We're getting no nearer identifying this monster."

I know. Her frustration echoed my own. "I need to get to the crime scene. Are you coming?"

"Yep. You're my ride."

I'd forgotten that. We'd barely been apart in waking hours. I offered her my hand and helped her to her feet. A minute later, we left the archives—and I didn't intend to return to them.

§

Parkside was another expensive area of town. I wouldn't be able to rent a garage there, let alone an apartment. But the earthquakes hadn't made any distinction between rich and poor. Buildings everywhere had been damaged, roads were ruined or potholed, and residents' nerves were frazzled.

It took us ten minutes to drive to the crime scene from the library with the news archives. My car's engine still sounded off; if cars could catch a cold, I'd say it had the 'flu. As before, patrol cars blocked the area off. We parked thirty metres away, my compact car dwarfed by prestigious SUVs around it. The earthy rumble of another minor aftershock greeted us as we exited the car.

It took a few minutes to convince the constable at the barrier tape to let us through. He didn't believe me that we were working with Inspector O'Toole and his team. Fortunately, the inspector arrived and ushered us past.

The coroner, Mikey Brown, was at the scene already with two constables and SOCOs. A large silver SUV, of the kind that school mums love because it passes over the potholes so gently, sat in the driveway of an elaborate two-storey house. Pillars at the entrance, although cracked, suggested affluence and prestige. But none of that mattered to the person in the car—and it was the car that the coroner was examining.

The driver's door was wide open. Inside, someone lay slumped on the seat, seatbelt fastened, head turned away. Or I should say some of the head was turned away. The rest of it was splattered over the windscreen, the passenger-side door, and the dashboard. The passenger-side window had been blown out.

Bile rose in my throat. Beside me, Deepa emitted a strangled choke, turned away and vomited into the gutter. O'Toole covered his mouth with a handkerchief.

"Death was instantaneous." Mikey was unperturbed. Of course, he was used to these scenes.

The inspector looked around as if hoping to see the murder weapon. No such luck. "Shotgun again?"

"Can't say for sure until we find the bullet or slug, and that could be anywhere down the street. I can tell you the killer shot her at point-blank range. She didn't have a chance."

"She?" My voice cracked.

"Yes. I can even tell you who she is. Her face is plastered on posters all over the city. It's Alice Hadwin, the talk-show host."

"Oh, damn. The killer phoned in last night." A sinking sensation swept through my stomach.

"Is that so?" Mikey raised an eyebrow.

"Yep." Deepa wiped her mouth with a tissue. "We had a run-in with them afterwards."

"We let the perp get away." I groaned. "If only we'd been fast enough, we'd have caught them."

"It's not our fault, Danny."

"Yes, it is. If we'd stopped the killer, Alice Hadwin would still be alive. She might have been a sensationalist radio hack playing the emotions of her audience like a harpsichord, but she didn't deserve this."

O'Toole scowled at us. "I had patrol cars out looking, but they didn't find anyone because you'd tipped the perp off that we were on to them."

Deepa stepped up close to O'Toole. Her eyes shone hard. "The killer was shooting at us. We had to give up the chase."

Mikey leaned forward and put his hand on my shoulder. "Don't blame yourself. You did all you could. Getting your own head blown off wouldn't help you catch the perp, would it?"

"Thanks, Mikey. I appreciate it." Coroner humour, I suppose.

"You should have kept following them so you could direct the patrol cars where to go." O'Toole wasn't finished grumbling.

I let it pass. Mikey was right. But I still felt some twinges of guilt. We needed to catch this monster before anyone else got murdered.

Deepa turned to face me, her back to the victim's car. "Where does this leave us? Can we draw any conclusions from Alice Hadwin's murder to help us with the investigation?"

"This is the killer's first female victim. That's significant, because the perp threatened Liz Nicholls and didn't shoot. I think they changed their mind at the last moment when she turned and they saw she was female. But now, if the perp's killing women too, they're even more dangerous and driven to kill than before."

"No, it's probably someone else." O'Toole dismissed my theory out of hand. "Different pattern, different killer. Standard profiling technique."

"I don't agree, Inspector. The killer is adapting, spreading out, struggling to contain their fury and urge to kill. There are links. Alice Hadwin was talking about the postmen murders."

"We've got multiple killers in action, Ashford. The circumstances are not the same as the other murders. It's someone else. A woman like this makes many enemies."

I fumed. I couldn't prove my theory yet, but I sensed I was right. It would be too much of a coincidence otherwise.

O'Toole kept on. "She's not a postwoman, is she? She doesn't deliver pamphlets in her spare time. Those are our killer's victims. She's a high-profile, wealthy individual known to most of the city. It's probably a robbery or carjacking gone wrong, and the killer panicked and fled. Or it could be another serial killer altogether."

"If you say so, Inspector."

"I do."

Deepa interrupted. "Danny, is there anything we can do here? Question witnesses? Let's not argue with the inspector." She rolled her eyes in such an exaggerated way that I found it hard not to smile. O'Toole didn't see it.

"You're right, Deepa. Thank you, Inspector. We'll carry on from here."

"Let me know if you come up with anything."

"Of course."

"You could try talking to the neighbour over there, at the ambulance. Janet

Quenton. She saw something."

At the ambulance, a woman sat with a blanket around her. An ambulance officer was assessing her for shock. She glanced up as we approached.

"You can't talk to her until I've finished, and then only briefly."

I nodded and we waited. It was about three o'clock, and the slight warmth of the day was already dissipating. After a few minutes, the ambulance officer allowed us to question her. I introduced us and said we were helping the police with enquiries. Deepa put her voice recorder on.

Janet Quenton was a smartly dressed woman in her fifties. Mascara streaked her cheeks.

"I heard a scream." Her voice trembled. "There was a loud bang—the shot—and I ran to the window. I saw the door slamming on a car parked in the street. Then it drove off quickly in that direction." She pointed south.

I inclined my head and spoke gently. "Can you describe the driver?"

"No. I couldn't see the driver's face because they kept their head down, and I was upstairs."

"Man or woman, even? Any description at all?"

"I couldn't tell. He or she wore a black beanie and jeans. I only got a glance before the car drove off."

"What kind of car was it?"

"A station wagon. Dark blue."

It's the same description as our killer's car. Almost certainly the same perpetrator. Why couldn't O'Toole see that?

Deepa got her attention. "Did the driver see you?" Perhaps she was worried about the witness' safety.

"No. They had their head down, like I said."

We questioned her a little longer but learned nothing more of importance. After thanking her and leaving her in the care of the ambulance officer, we updated O'Toole. Two or three constables were searching for damage further down the road, looking for the ultimate resting place of the bullet or slug. It could be anywhere.

Then we took our leave before I got into another argument with O'Toole. He was being pig-headed, unable to see a point of view other than his own.

Chapter 28

DEEPA AND I REGROUPED at the Cracked Up café by the river in Crashmere over late afternoon coffees. Deepa, however, wasn't drinking hers. She tipped little bags of sugar into the cup, played with the teaspoon, then gave me a pained look.

Finally, she spoke. "The murders are getting more horrid, aren't they?"

"Yes. The killer's more disturbed, more hateful. Maybe working up to something worse."

"Worse than shooting an innocent woman in the head?"

"Possibly. I can't be sure, but it's might be the perp's daring themselves more each time. Ricky Cohen was a drive-by shooting at a distance. With Alice Hadwin, the killer got out of their car and shot her at point-blank range."

"I see what you mean."

"So… maybe the killer has some ultimate, elaborate murder in mind, and these are—"

"Merely warm-ups. That's a horrible thought."

"Killers like that place no value on human life. The people they kill as 'practice' are nothing to them. If that's what the perp's doing."

"What a sicko."

"I'm not saying this is definitely what's happening. It might explain what we're seeing with the change in M.O., though."

"You mean, not killing people delivering stuff to mailboxes?"

"Yes, and attacking a woman at close range, like I said. But it still ties in with the messengers theme. She gave messages, too, but over the airwaves."

"Not anymore." Deepa's face was grim. Her eyes opened wide. "Does this mean I'm in danger? Alice was killed because of her talk show last night, wasn't she?"

I nodded. It couldn't be a coincidence.

"I've been writing about the killer every day. Shit! The monster will target me next."

"Try to relax. The killer might not read the newspaper, and therefore wouldn't know anything about you." I couldn't know that. My gut tightened as I weighed the possibility that the perp already had Deepa in his sights.

"There's no way to be sure, though, is there?"

"No, there isn't." I contemplated what I would say next. "Deepa, how would you like to spend the night at my place again?"

"Oh, yep, please. I'm so glad you asked."

A while later, Deepa paid for the drinks, and then we left. We drove in silence, both of us absorbed in our own thoughts. I had no idea what was in Deepa's mind, but mine was racing.

This was becoming a habit. If you can call two consecutive nights a habit. I'd have to sleep on the sofa again, and fight Torquemada for enough space to stretch out, while Deepa slept in the bed. My bed.

This would not be a long-term solution.

Of course she didn't want to go home. If the killer *did* read the *Richter Mail*, they would know of her. Some basic research would provide them with her address. Having seen what the perp had done to Alice Hadwin for talking about the murders, Deepa was visibly nervous about being home alone. So, she'd chosen to stay with me instead.

But why? Did she have no one else to stay with? After all, she'd written about me as well: the 'great detective' who would solve the case and save the city, according to her. Could I do it? Find a crazed serial killer before they kill more people, seemingly targeted at random? I couldn't even prevent Torquemada from scratching the sofa.

And, because Deepa had written about me too, the killer knew my name and could find my address. Would she be any safer here with me? The killer could come here and shoot both of us. That's if they got past Mrs Werther.

Or did Deepa have another reason for staying with me? Could I allow myself this thought? Would anything come of it?

Get a grip. We're working together; she needs me to provide profiling and opinion, and to investigate the case so she can write and sell her articles. When this was all over, our working partnership would lapse and the only contact I'd have with Deepa would be through her inked words on the pages of the *Richter Mail*.

"You all right, Danny?" Her smooth voice cut through my ragged inner thoughts.

"Got a lot on my mind. Let's stop for dinner. I'll buy."

"Excellent idea. Not McDonald's again, though?"

"Of course not."

I took Deepa to Quake Burgers. She ordered a vegetarian thing I'd never even noticed was on the menu. I had a proper burger, side of fries, drink—the usual.

"You'll make yourself fat if that's all you eat." She gestured to my food once we'd sat.

"Maybe."

"You won't be able to chase after criminals. They'll be faster than you."

"Most of my work is covert. I don't have to chase after anyone."

"Why not eat healthier? It'll be better for you in the long run."

What do you care? I almost said it, but held back. My grumpiness and frustration weren't only because of our lack of progress with the case, but the investigation was all I was willing to talk about.

I changed the subject. "Our killer is a very private person. Most likely male. The perp probably lives alone, or possibly with a parent. They will have struggled with relationships. The perp's below average intelligence and probably works for themselves, seeing as they seem to be able to pick times and places as they want."

Deepa grabbed her notebook and flipped it open. "How do you know this?"

"Profiling. And I've been thinking about this a lot. There's more. The killer doesn't think about evidence left behind, or doesn't care. Remember the tyre print in the Red Zone. On the other hand, there isn't much evidence for us to go on."

Deepa scribbled flat out while eating with her other hand.

I ate some of my burger while I got my thoughts in order, then continued. "The perp's not completely disorganised, though. The murders aren't all purely random. Alice Hadwin was deliberately targeted, so that suggests that some of the earlier murders might not have been random either."

"I don't get it. So, the killer's neither organised nor disorganised? Is that what you're saying? I can't write a statement that vague."

"Yes. The killer is between those extremes. That's good for us, as they might make mistakes, and it also gives us angles to investigate. Now we know the perp hates people talking about them, for instance."

"That's not making me feel any better, Danny." Deepa shuddered, her pen skidding across the page.

"I understand you feeling that way, but we can't ignore that fact. It'll help us narrow down a list of suspects."

"We don't *have* any suspects."

"Let's take our original list and narrow it down some more. I think we were on the right track: someone with a psychiatric disorder who's been triggered into violent action by something that we haven't yet uncovered. But now we know more about our murderer, we should have another look at that list."

"Right, because you don't want to go back to the news archives and search there any longer."

She was right—I didn't. Sure, we might find something in there that led us to the killer, but it wasn't likely. "The traumatic event in the killer's past, if there even is one, could be a personal trauma rather than a newsworthy event. I think we were wasting our time there."

"Of course you do. You got bored looking through the archives. You'd much sooner be racing around town in your zippy car."

Yes, but I wouldn't admit it. "Aren't the archives closed for the day now?"

Deepa frowned. "Yep, they are."

"Then when we're back at the office, let's look at our list again, or make a new list based on the profile I've come up with."

"But surely interviewing people at random isn't a constructive use of our time? You're relying on Fate to put the killer in our path."

I didn't answer at first, taking time to tidy up the food wrappings and containers and put them on the plastic tray. I didn't want to argue with Deepa, but it was hard not to as she was so argumentative. I wanted to pursue the investigation the way I needed to—my way. Even if it wasn't efficient. "If I interview someone and learn they cannot be the killer, I can rule them out. That's useful information."

"All right. Let's do it your way. You're the private investigator, after all." She paused. "It's been a hard day. Maybe we should take the evening off. I'll go for a run. You could visit your daughter or something."

"You take the evening off if you want. A conscientious private investigator never rests while there's a case to investigate. I'll go through the police databases and make a new list of people to interview."

Would the killer strike again before I could find them?

My stomach churned with the thought.

Chapter 29

I GOT HER GOOD. The bitch wouldn't shut up when I told her, so I waited for her and got her good. Half her head blown off. She'll keep her fucking mouth shut now.

The rush when I did it is to die for. Oh fuck, yes, it's hot. A hot rush. Blows my mind with ecstasy. And the funny thing, oh the funny thing is that it was her mind that was blown across the car. Fucking cool.

The feel of the cold metal gun. The sighting of my target. The look on her face when she realizes I'm the last person she'll ever see. The booming of the shot echoing inside the car. The smell of sulphur. It's the best. It's the hottest thing in the world.

Do it again. Do it again. Do it again.

Wait, though. I'm off track. That bitch was an exception. She wouldn't keep her mouth shut on the radio. Now, I gotta get back on track. Back on target.

Yeah, more targets.

They deliver messages of hate. They come in the house. They come in my room. Wait. Is that right?

It must be, because that's why I have to stop them. Fucking stop them all.

Yeah. That's right. Fucking get another one, then.

Chapter 30

Day 6, morning

MY REVISED, SLIMMER LIST of potentials lay on the passenger seat of my car as I drove. I'd tightened my search criteria in the police database a little more, then weeded out those whose profile didn't fit my idea of the killer. If I'd not done that, I'd never be able to interview everyone on the list. And I didn't want to cool my heels at the news archives, where Deepa had gone.

Worry gnawed at my gut. I'd reduced my list to a manageable size, but by eliminating so many suspects, had I crossed out the name of the killer?

I shook my head, trying to dispel the unease, but it wouldn't go. Was there something I'd missed? Something I'd seen but not realised was important at the time? Some shortcut to the investigation that might save lives?

There was no way to know.

I parked in a tree-lined street in Crumbledon outside an old rickety villa. What was once a brick chimney lay shattered in the garden on one side of the house, a casualty of the last major earthquake like virtually every other chimney in the city. Santa Claus would need a lock pick. Part of a low brick wall separating the property from the street lay in its adjacent flowerbed, though the flowerbed in question was nothing more than a bare patch of earth with four old car tyres in it.

The gate was shut, so I stepped over the collapsed wall and approached the front door.

Jake Munro answered the door after my third knock, when he'd probably worked out that I wasn't going away. He was tall with a trim, neat beard, a buttoned-up shirt, and a smart suit. He was a regular in the police station, but wasn't always so well dressed.

"Who are you?" Jake stared at me. At least he didn't slam the door in my face.

I told him and flashed my PI's ID. "Just routine questions, Jake. I'm interviewing people on behalf of the police to eliminate them from the investigation." The lie slipped out so easily due to frequent use.

He didn't fall for it. "Yeah, right. Something happens and you guys are banging on my door, ready to pin it on me when I don't even know anything about it."

"It's not personal, Jake. I'm checking up on lots of people. You're known to the police. Do you mind telling me if you own a shotgun?" I might as well be direct. I didn't have time to mess around. He'd once beaten up a businesswoman. I needed to know if he was capable of murder and in the current frame of mind to commit it.

"A shotgun? No, that's never been my style, Detective."

Naturally, he'd say that. "I'm not a detective, Jake, I'm a private investigator. You got a job interview or something?"

"No. Why?"

I nodded at his attire. "You're dressed up like an estate agent."

"I—I'm going to church."

I frowned. "On a weekday?"

"Look, it's not against the law to dress smartly, is it?"

"No, of course not. But I know you're on the sickness benefit, like you were when you got into trouble last time, conning people out of deposits for rental properties by pretending to be a letting agent."

"Well, that was a long time ago. Look, what the hell do you want, apart from mocking my clothes?"

"How about you show me your wheels? You drive a station wagon, don't you?"

"I do. How do you know?"

"I know things. Is it in the garage there, Jake?" I inclined my head towards the single garage alongside the fence line.

"Yeah, it's in there. Do you have a warrant?"

I shook my head. "No warrant. This is just a friendly enquiry."

"I don't have to show you anything if you don't have a warrant. Go get one." He sneered. "Oh, you can't do that, because you're not police, are you? So, you're out of luck."

"I can get the police to come back with a warrant and tear your place apart."

Jake lifted his chin and sneered. "I doubt that. They would've come themselves if they'd wanted. Besides, they're only interested in those murders, and I've nothing to do with those. But if they do come—and that's a big 'if'—they'll be wasting their time. There's nothing to find."

Yeah, exactly. Any evidence will be long gone by then. "You're not being very cooperative, Jake. How about telling me where you were yesterday morning?"

"I don't remember. I'm a busy guy. And innocent. I've been keeping out of trouble. How about you get off my property now?"

He stared at me until I turned, went back to the car and drove off.

§

Gary Stone was next on my list. Again, I had no more reason to suspect him than that he owned a station wagon and had had episodes of violence. Him and dozens, if not hundreds, of other people, but I'd limited my search to those who lived in the area of the first murders.

It was ten minutes' drive. Stone lived in Dumpsbury. He had a stint in a secure mental health ward following robbery and assault when he was manic. But from the look of his house, he'd bounced back and made something of his life. More than I had, anyway.

Stone wasn't home. I rechecked the information I had from the printout of my shortlist from the police database. He had a job as a representative of a pharmaceutical company, going from store to store with stocks of prescription drugs. I wondered if he helped himself to some of them from time to time.

He could be anywhere. I phoned his company and asked them. After much wheedling, flattery and downright lying, I managed to persuade someone to

117

tell me where his next appointment was. It was ten minutes' drive away in Crumbledon, in five minutes' time.

I drove there, bouncing over more potholes than usual because of my haste, and parked in the carpark of a mall. All the malls look the same to me, and they're all big enough that finding any particular store isn't a trivial task. Especially when you're already late.

The pharmacy hove into view as I strode through the mall, my heels clicking on the cracked tile floor. A figure with a case bearing the name of the pharmaceutical company Gary Stone worked for stepped out. I stopped him and introduced myself, then ushered him to the side of the concourse.

"I don't have much time. I have another appointment." He made an exaggerated check of his watch.

"I won't take up much of your time, Gary." I lowered my voice and studied him carefully. "Do you mind telling me if you own a shotgun, by any chance?"

"What? No. And before you ask, I've been straight for years now, ever since… the troubles I had when I was younger."

I nodded. "Looks like you got yourself a pretty decent job for someone with a criminal record."

His mouth opened, shut, and opened again. "Some people are willing to give others a second chance."

Or he lied on his application. Either way, that wasn't the issue. He seemed stable. Perhaps his medication worked wonders, and any manic episodes were long past. "You drive a station wagon, Gary?"

"I own one, but it's at home. I'm in the company car today. A little Honda Civic. That's all I need around town anyway. Do you have any more questions? I need to get going."

I wanted to ask him if he'd been shooting postmen and talk-show hosts, but I'm usually subtler than that. "Were you working yesterday, driving the company car?"

"Yes. All day, in fact. Here, take a look." He pulled an iPhone from his pocket and showed me a calendar app. Appointments at stores all over town, all week, including yesterday.

"Thank you, Gary. That's all for now. You've been very helpful."

He rushed off without saying goodbye. I waited for a bit, then followed him at a discreet distance. He got into a Honda Civic with the logo of his company on it.

I wanted to rule him out, but I couldn't. With two cars, and a job that allowed him to travel freely around the city, it would have been possible for him to switch cars when he was in the area, murder someone, then switch back before continuing on with his list of appointments. Was he capable? Possibly. He had the opportunity. Maybe the killer can hide themselves in society well.

Chapter 31

Day 6, afternoon

IT WAS TIME TO CALL Deepa. I fished my phone from my pocket, checked I still had credit, and made the call.

She answered immediately. "Hey, there. Any luck?"

"Not really. One cooperative and one uncooperative. I can't rule either of them out. How are you doing?"

She sighed. "I'm using all my research tricks to go through the archives as quickly and thoroughly as I can. There's nothing so far. But I sense that I'll find something here."

"What, though?" Deepa was doing better than me. Was I wasting my time?

"A traumatic event that was recently triggered, like you said. I just need to keep looking."

"Want to get some lunch?"

"Sure, but no burgers this time. How about sandwiches?"

I agreed to go where she wanted. If I didn't like it, I could always get a burger afterwards. We'd arranged to meet at the place.

I walked back to my car. A police officer stood in front of it, entering details into a hand-held device that resulted in a letter demanding payment of a fine, delivered, ironically, by post.

This was the last thing I needed. I fronted up to the officer. "What's that for?"

"Your busted headlight." The officer didn't even look up.

I fumed. "Shouldn't you be doing something more important? There's a serial killer on the loose. Why aren't you out searching for them instead of issuing vehicle fines?"

He glanced up. If there was any empathy in his expression, I didn't see it. "Not my department. I'm in revenue generation, the team who get the money to keep the city's police department operating."

"I know what they do. Listen, give me a break here. I'm a private investigator. I'm on your side. And for your information, the killer you're not looking for shot out that headlight. Can't you let me off?"

"Quotas. Targets. Revenue. Sorry you don't like it." He closed his device and walked off.

My skin prickling with annoyance, I got in the car. It drove like sandpaper on gravel, the engine coughing and spluttering like its mechanical cold was getting worse.

I met Deepa at the sandwich place a few minutes away. She was already seated, and she smiled when I came through the door. My irritation melted like cheese under a hot grill.

"I bought you this." She pointed to something on a plate opposite her seat. She had the same in front of her. "It's gluten-free bread with salad, tofu and cress, full of nutritional goodness."

"Is it actually food?" I eyed it dubiously.

"Of course it is." She took a big bite out of her one.

I took a hesitant bite out of mine. It tasted like nothing. In some small way, it reminded me of how we were getting on with the investigation.

§

Deepa returned to her beloved news archives after our lunch, determined to prove—to me and to herself—that a hidden clue lay in the past on those old microfiches or digital records, and all she had to do was find it to uncover the killer's motive and identity.

I thought the chance of that was slim. And it's not how a sharp private investigator works. It's not how I work.

Mind you, I hadn't gotten anywhere either. While she delved through old news reports, I sat in the Shake, Rattle and Roll café in Baddington, thinking about the case. Stewing like old filter coffee. Soon, I'd be bitter too.

I must have missed something. Someone had lied, or forgotten some trivial detail that would crack the case wide open.

It was one o'clock. I went outside and phoned Dave at the NZ Post depot, hoping he wasn't out to lunch. He picked up the call after a single ring.

"Dave, it's Danny Ashcroft here."

"Danny, any news?"

"Not yet." I shook my head, despite Dave being unable to see that. At the same time, I chided myself for not driving out to the depot and talking to him in person. He was still in the back of my mind as a suspect. "Help me out here. Ricky Cohen and Chris Dodd—could they have been involved in anything together? A business gone bad, for instance?"

"No, nothing of that kind. I already told you. They both kept to themselves most of the time, as far as I know. But I'm glad you called. I have a problem. Another of my postal workers has gone missing. Annette Graves."

The mention of her surname made my heart miss a beat. Graves. What an unfortunate name in the context of what was going on. "Missing? How do you know she's missing?"

"She abandoned her postal cart two-thirds of the way through her route. Obviously, that's forbidden, so I immediately thought something was wrong. A… a family emergency, or…"

I didn't press him to finish the sentence. I already knew what he couldn't bring himself to say.

"She's not answering her phone. I sent someone round to her house, but she's not there either. I would call the police, but she's only been missing for an hour…" Dave groaned.

"Do you have a photo of her?"

"Yes, on file. I'll ask Jasmine to text it to you."

"Thanks. Try not to worry." For now. "Annette may turn up. Maybe her phone's out of battery."

"Maybe." Dave didn't sound convinced. "Some of my employees are refusing to work, saying it's too dangerous with that madman on the loose. Maybe Annette abandoned her route because of that. Can't say I blame them, but it'll be a massive disruption to mail delivery across the city."

As if anyone would notice the difference. "Leave it with me."

I disconnected, then phoned O'Toole with that information. He growled for a few seconds before ending the call. My guess is he would not take much notice of a person missing for only an hour, even when they fit the profile of our killer's victims. It wouldn't match the previous murders, where the perp had shot someone on the spot, even if he'd moved the body later like Chris Dodd. If he had taken Annette Graves, we had no idea where to look.

Nevertheless, a sense of dread flooded through me. Was Graves the perp's next scalp?

A text came through. The photo of Annette. An outdoorsy, weather-beaten type, maybe in her forties. Nothing like the other victims.

Dammit. I was already thinking of her as dead.

The phone rang. O'Toole again. I answered it. "Yes, Inspector?"

"New initiative. I will make a public appeal for information on the six o'clock news tonight. We'll have every constable we can gather manning the phones. Seeing as you're working on the case too, I need you here for that, helping to screen out time-wasters and attention-seekers."

He hadn't bothered to ask nicely. I reached up under my hat and scratched my head. "There'll be plenty of those, Inspector. Are you sure it's a sensible idea?"

"No, but the superintendent wants it. She's breathing down my neck on this one. Said we're nowhere with it and we need to try something new, so this is it, what she wanted."

"Right." The superintendent wouldn't be one of the ones manning the phones or screening the callers. She'd be out at the opera or some charity dinner and wouldn't have to listen to the blathering diatribes of rot that some callers come up with.

Looks like I was in for another evening when I wouldn't have time to visit my daughter.

Chapter 32

Day 6, evening

SIX O'CLOCK ROLLED AROUND. I'd arrived at the police station about five o'clock to help with the setup and meet everyone. Sergeant Amy Ling was in charge of proceedings. Deepa was downstairs, amongst other reporters waiting for the appeal to take place on live television and radio.

I'd spent the afternoon looking for Annette Graves. Her postal route, her home, her kids' play centre, her mother's house. All drew a blank. What had happened to her? Worry gnawed at me like a beaver at wood.

Constables hovered over phones. We all watched proceedings on an enormous TV screen as Inspector O'Toole took his seat and started to read from a pre-prepared speech.

"Good evening. An evil perpetrator has committed heinous crimes in our city…"

The inspector went on to describe the murders in far more detail than the majority of viewers would want to hear. He appealed for witnesses who hadn't already come forward, and for anyone with any suspicions whatsoever, to contact the police on a dedicated number, which then appeared on television screens nationwide.

Within moments, phones started going off.

One by one, constables picked up a ringing phone. Amy stood watching them like a conductor temporarily frozen in motion. I joined her.

A young female constable, Debbie, beckoned. "Sergeant, this one claims to have seen the killer every time."

That's extremely unlikely, I thought.

"I'll check it out." Amy went over to speak to the caller.

I approached Peter, who was talking to another caller about the car. He pointed at the phone, then handed it to me. "Sounds genuine."

What information did the caller have? I took the phone from Peter and spoke into it. "Do you mind repeating what you just told the constable?"

"I said, I live in the same street as where that pensioner was killed." The caller was male, possibly aged. "I heard the shot, then I saw a navy-blue station wagon driving past at speed."

"Did you report this on the day?"

"No one asked me."

I took a deep breath, then exhaled. "Did you see the driver clearly?"

"I think it was a woman, white, under thirty, I'd say."

"A woman? Are you sure?"

"No, I can't say for sure. The car was going damned fast."

"Hair colour?"

"They wore a brown cap."

"Would you recognise them again?"

"Probably not. I only glimpsed them in profile for a moment."

"Okay. Thanks." I gave the phone back to Peter and went over to update Amy. She was hanging up on a caller at that moment. "Any good?"

She shook her head. "This guy claimed the CIA is behind the murders."

Debbie called out. "Russians over here."

Another constable slammed a phone down. "The North Koreans." We chuckled, despite the situation.

I told Amy about the updated description, that the caller thought the driver was a woman. Or said he thought the driver was a woman. Though of course we didn't know if the car and driver were the ones in question anyway.

Sam beckoned, and I went over. "This caller says the killer abducted him. He won't give his name. I thought he should talk to you."

I took the phone. "Tell me what happened."

"It was yesterday. Yeah, yesterday morning. I'd left the bottle store and this big guy with crazy eyes grabbed me from behind in the car park. He had one of them A3 semi-automatic guns and jabbed the barrel into my back. Then—"

"Wait. How do you know it was an A3?"

"I saw it later. I'm getting there. He hit me on the head with it and knocked me out. Then he stuffed me into the back of a big SUV."

"And you saw that later, too, right? Because you were unconscious at the time."

The caller hesitated. I shook my head to Sam, indicating that I thought the caller was another attention seeker. He set up a trace on the call.

"I woke up in the back of the car. The guy took me to a big house somewhere—don't know where—and pulled me from the boot of the car. I'd untied myself by then—"

"You didn't say he'd tied you up."

"Well, he did. Anyway, I punched him. Knocked him clean out with one hit. Then I searched his car and found the AK47. And I thought, I could do the country a favour by shooting this guy right here, right now."

"But you didn't, did you? And you just said the gun's an AK47. Before, it was an A3."

"He had one of each. A real military type of guy. Tough, you know. But I knocked him out cold. I should get a medal."

I made a circular motion by the side of my head, indicating to Sam and Amy, who were both watching, what I thought of the caller's state of mind. "And then why didn't you call the police, if you'd just captured the infamous serial killer on your own?"

"I—uh—I thought someone would come along and do that. I wanted to get back to my car. See if my beer was okay or if some bastard had stolen it."

"How did you get home?"

Pause. "I called a taxi."

"Even though you didn't know where you were. And the taxi driver obviously didn't see the unconscious serial killer lying on the ground when they picked you up."

"Don't you believe me? Typical."

Sam gave a thumbs-up about tracing the call. Time to end it. "What you deserve is to be charged for wasting police time on this investigation. Expect a visit from a constable later." I hung up.

The phones kept ringing. False witnesses. Four people confessed to being the killer themselves—one was aged eighty-two. Amy dispatched patrol cars to bring them all in, but from what they'd said over the phone, they were attention-seeking time-wasters.

I didn't see when Inspector O'Toole came into the briefing room, but I noticed him answering phones too. He must be anxious to make progress if he was deigning to take calls himself.

Debbie stood and waved her hand in a circular motion, indicating her call was urgent. She put the call on speakerphone so we could all hear, then continued talking. "Repeat what you just told me, caller."

"I know who the killer is. His name's Gerry."

It was a woman's voice but disguised or muffled somehow, as if the caller had covered her mouth with a cloth.

I replied. "What's your name? How do we know you're for real? How do we know you're not a crank caller? There've been plenty of those tonight."

"Gerry's got a postwoman with him. Her name's Annette something."

Chapter 33

A WALL OF ICE HIT ME at the core. Around me, everyone listening reacted with a gasp, an open mouth, or widening eyes.

Debbie mouthed that she was getting a GPS fix on the caller's mobile phone.

I talked slowly, to give Debbie time to track the call, and to try to keep the caller calm. "How do you know this? Does Gerry have you hostage too?"

"Gerry doesn't know I'm calling you. Gerry is very sick, and he's not listening at the moment."

"Where are you? Can you escape? Can you and Annette get out of there?"

"Not possible. Gerry is listening now."

Debbie scribbled on a notepad: "The phone belongs to Annette Graves."

"Listen, we want to help you—"

A new voice came on the phone. Deeper, stronger. "Stop trying to find me. Get those fucking reporters to stop writing about me. Anyone who does that becomes my target. Got it, arseholes?"

My breathing became shallower and quicker, hyperventilating. Deepa was right to be afraid—she was a target! My head felt lighter.

I took a deep breath. Pull yourself together, Danny.

O'Toole leaned in. If he leaned much further, he'd probably overbalance. "You need psychiatric help. We can give that to you. Simply let Annette and that other woman go, and tell us your location. I guarantee you won't be harmed if you give yourself up quietly."

The killer laughed. Long and hard. In his maniacal laughter, I detected hilarity at the idea of giving himself up. Scorn at the naivety of the inspector's demands. And, worse, a deep-seated cruel enjoyment of the situation.

"Got their location yet?" O'Toole asked Debbie. She shook her head. I winced. We needed it. Quickly.

"Why are you doing this?" I needed to keep the killer on the line. Maybe it would keep Annette alive. And whoever the caller was who wouldn't give her name.

"The TV."

"What about the TV, Gerry?" I shivered, despite the sweat beading on my forehead.

"I'm only doing what it tells me."

I chose my words with care. "Television programmes are speaking to you?"

"Not the programmes. The ads. Clean up. Goodbye to bad memories. Rinse and repeat."

My mouth dried at the deep voice and crazy words.

Debbie stabbed the 'mute' button. "I've got it. He's in Ricketyton. In the mall carpark building."

Amy raced to a desk. She put a call through to dispatch patrol cars.

Debbie unmuted the phone. I needed to keep the perp talking. "Will you tell us your last name, Gerry?"

"No can do."

O'Toole grabbed the phone from me. "What have the ads been telling you to do next, Gerry?"

My stomach clenched. That might prompt the killer into action instead of more talk.

"This." The sound of a car door opening came through the phone. Then scuffling. Then the sound of tape tearing off something.

I ground my teeth.

The inspector huffed. "What are you doing, Gerry?"

A woman screamed down the line, a terrifying, mind-chilling scream. It lasted only a few moments before a loud blast terminated it. The discharge of a shotgun.

The call cut off. O'Toole shouted orders. I wasn't listening. I ran out of the office and down the stairs two at a time.

Two patrol cars raced past me when I emerged onto the footpath.

Deepa joined me as I ran to my Swift and jumped inside. She slipped onto the front passenger seat and plonked her bag on the floor. "What's going on, Danny?"

I gunned the engine of my Swift, hoping to tail the patrol cars blazing the way with their sirens blaring, but they were already out of sight. I took off in pursuit. The engine screamed in protest, and I ignored it.

"The killer's in Ricketyton. He called us. I'll tell you about it on the way. I think he just shot Annette Graves."

"Oh, shit."

"There's more." I filled her in.

It was usually a ten-minute drive, but I was aiming for under seven minutes.

"Hurry." Deepa, no stranger to speeding, waved at the road, impatient. "Your car must be able to go faster than this."

I slowed for a red light. The intersection was clear. I accelerated through it. "The killer was in the mall car park and may have dragged Annette from the car and killed her. Sounded like it over the phone. There's another woman with him. A second hostage? Maybe he's killed her too. And he would have left the car park by now and be getting away."

"The patrol cars might trap him. If they don't, we'll be too late anyway."

"He might slip past them." I overtook a slow car by Tower Junktown. We were less than two minutes away. "Look out for a navy-blue station wagon."

"With no clear description of the driver." Deepa groaned.

"He might look anxious or flushed, or even bloodstained. Use your intuition. Someone fleeing from a murder scene surely must look different from someone going about their normal business."

Deepa scanned the traffic coming our way. A truck bearing a full-size container took up most of the width of the other side of the road, blocking our view. I raced past it in the other direction, towards the mall.

"I think that was it, tailgating the truck." Deepa swivelled in her seat to look at the car receding into the distance behind us.

I had seen nothing. Obviously, the patrol cars hadn't either. We were lucky that Deepa was observant.

I braked hard, the tyres protesting with a shriek, and swung the car around. Horns blared.

Deepa braced herself on the dashboard. "I can still see the car. It's gone through the lights back at Tower Junktown."

"Did you get the number plate?"

"No."

"Get a clear view of the driver?"

"No."

Dammit. The lights had changed to red by the time I reached them, but I didn't let that stop me. Pulse pounding, I hammered my horn. I slowed enough to avoid a collision, then accelerated again through a small gap in the turning traffic. Would the station wagon be stuck at the next major intersection? There'd be no threading my way through the four lanes of traffic there.

"I can't see it." Deepa threw her hands in the air. "No knowing where it went."

I pulled over. It could have gone left or right, then onto any of several side streets, or straight ahead, with options of turning onto the highway in either direction. "The perp's gotten away. Again. Hell's teeth!"

"We should go back to the mall."

Something occurred to me. "Did you see anyone else in the car?"

"I really didn't get a good enough look to know either way."

The other hostage could have been in the back, lying on the floor. But that didn't seem right. Why would the killer kidnap two people, one of whom we hadn't yet identified as missing, then shoot one of them? It didn't fit any of the previous killings. In fact, a lot of it didn't fit. Who was the unknown woman on the phone? What happened to her?

"Of course, that might not have been the killer's car." Deepa sounded thoughtful, the tension in her voice faded now. "There are a lot of dark-blue station wagons around."

"Let's get to the mall and see what's happened there." Although I already knew it would be a crime scene. My skin crawled with the thought.

We turned around and drove to the mall more sedately, at the speed limit.

Deepa's face was grim. I stayed silent. We both knew what we'd find there.

We parked nearby. The two patrol cars had blocked the road leading to the mall on this side. More sirens sounded in the distance, approaching the scene.

There was no one to stop us. Two police officers stood by the greenery at the bottom of the mall's car parking building. There would be two others somewhere, perhaps at the entrance to the car park.

We ran over. I showed my PI license, and Deepa flashed her press card. One of the constables recognised me and let us through once I convinced him we were working with Inspector O'Toole.

The postwoman, Annette Graves, lay in the flax bushes, hands bound with a cable tie in front of her, eyes staring at the sky. Blood soaked her uniform and the grass. She'd been shot in the chest at close range, and I'd wager the weapon was a shotgun. Killed instantly, by the look of it.

I glanced up. Maybe the killer had shot her on the open-air parking level above, and she fell over the balcony. Or maybe it happened at ground level, behind the flax bushes. Either way, the killer was audacious, reckless, and yet had gotten away again.

Deepa wasn't looking. I assumed she wanted to avoid being sick again. My breathing quickened, my chest tightened, and I cursed myself for failing to stop the killer before yet another needless death.

The constable withdrew some ID from a purse on the ground and spoke to me. "This says her name is Annette Graves. We think she fell from the first or second level. There were no footprints or evidence of movement in the foliage here when we arrived."

"All right. Thanks, guys."

Another police car pulled up. O'Toole got out of it. I nodded grimly to him and returned to my car, Deepa with me. I pulled the door closed, jammed the key into the ignition, but I didn't feel like driving. Instead, I rested my head on the steering wheel, eyes closed, my mind going over everything, waiting for my pulse to return to normal.

Deepa gazed at me intensely. "What's wrong, Danny? Other than the obvious, I mean."

I sat up. "When Gerry spoke on the appeals line, he said that television advertisements were speaking directly to him, telling him what to do. He didn't say it, but I'm sure he meant that they were telling him to kill people."

"Sure. He's a psycho, isn't he?"

I didn't respond. Deepa reached out and lay a hand on my shoulder. "What else?"

"O'Toole asked Gerry what the ads had been telling him to do next. He shot Annette a few seconds later."

"Shit. You mean O'Toole might have triggered him into killing the postwoman?"

"We can't know for sure, but it's possible. Maybe it made no difference. He was probably going to kill her anyway. But if we'd kept him on the phone for another few minutes..."

"Do you think he's so stupid that he'd phone the police appeals line and then wait for them to come and arrest him?"

"He didn't come across as someone who's playing with a full deck of cards. And he's getting more and more reckless."

"Is that a good or a bad thing?"

Deepa's hand still rested on my shoulder. It was comforting, and I wasn't about to shake it off. "Could be either. If he's more reckless, he'll make mistakes and we'll be more likely to catch him. On the downside, his crimes might be more frequent and even worse."

"Worse than killing people?"

"This is the first time he's kidnapped someone and then killed them later. It's a new twist. Maybe even torture is on his bucket list for the future."

Deepa paled and withdrew her supportive hand. She hugged herself. A fleeting thought of me hugging her passed through my mind. "What a terrible idea."

I jolted as if she was reacting to my internal thought rather than to what I had said. "We simply don't know exactly what is in his sick, twisted mind." Actually, my experience and my amateur study of forensic psychology gave me a fair idea of the evil thoughts he might be having, and they weren't pretty.

"My scooter's at the police station on Crumblo Street. Can you drive me back there, please?"

"Sure." I turned the key. The Swift burst into life. It was a zippy wee about-town thing. I liked it a lot, which is why I hadn't bought an expensive petrol-guzzling high-powered vehicle more suited to a bad-ass private investigator.

But, at the moment, it wasn't zipping like it should be. It sounded hideously rough.

We drove for a while until I broke the silence. "What's your next article about, Deepa?"

She groaned. "The deadline for tomorrow's edition has passed already. I missed it. Don, the editor at the *Richter Mail*, told me readers want to know more about the murders and the killer's profile, not read obituaries of the victims' lives. I'll write an article tomorrow."

"A grisly readership." I turned into Crumblo Street, the city's longest street, which runs north and south of the red-zoned Central Busted District.

"Yeah, well, I spent nearly all day in the news archives for nothing. What a waste of time, just like you said."

"Sorry for giving you a hard time about that. But, as it turns out, you might be right after all. The killer—and he called himself Gerry, but I doubt that's his actual name—said television ads were telling him to kill, to erase awful memories."

"Really? So, there must be something in his past."

"Yes. It might not be in the news archives, though. It might be personal. We can't possibly know at this point."

Deepa became silent. I parked the car outside the police station, metres from her scooter.

She turned to face me. "Danny, I don't want to go home. That bastard knows I've been writing about him. Look what happened to Alice Hadwin. I'm frightened."

The Messenger Shooter was the subject of many other reporters' stories, but I didn't point that out. Deepa's fear was genuine. He'd demanded that reporters stop writing about him. I'd never forgive myself if I ignored that and something happened to Deepa. The very thought of it chilled me to the core.

"So… I was thinking I should stay in a motel or something."

Ah. The 'something' was probably my place. "You don't have to stay in a motel, Deepa. You're welcome to stay over at mine again. If you feel safe there. Torquemada's a wonderful guard cat."

"Oh, thanks, Danny." She leaned towards me, and I thought she was going to kiss me for a moment, but she only smiled, and then she swung herself out of the car. "See you later, alligator." She grabbed the bag with her laptop.

"Sure. In a while—" I curtailed the expected response. It was too corny. Besides, Deepa had already shut the car door and gone. I chided myself for being stupid.

Working out what she was thinking was proving as difficult as solving the case itself.

Chapter 34

WHEN I REACHED HOME, despite trying to creep up the stairs avoiding the creakiest steps, I failed to get past Mrs Werther. She ambushed me as soon as I stepped foot on the landing, bustling out of her apartment, wearing a big red cardigan with the sleeves rolled up as if she meant business. She wanted to know how everything was going. The glint in her eye told me she wasn't talking about the investigation.

I answered as if she was. "I'm working on it, Mrs Werther." I tried to edge past, but she moved to block me.

"And how is that pretty young friend of yours?"

"We work together. Nothing more." Why did I feel so grumpy? Tired? Annoyed by being waylaid by my nosy neighbour?

"Oh-ho. You can't pull the wool over my eyes, you know. I've seen too much young love in my day to be fooled."

I took a deep breath before replying. "Mrs Werther, we're chasing leads on a case together. That's all. And it's really not your business anyway. Now, if you don't mind, I have to… to… to go inside and feed Torquemada."

"Hmph." She frowned and moved aside a little. I squeezed past, walked down the hall to my apartment, and unlocked the door. Once inside, I let out the huge breath I'd been holding in. Neighbours!

I fed Torquemada, then lay on the sofa, with the cat curled up against me, to think about the phone call on the appeals line. The killer must have had the radio on in his car. But who was the caller? What happened to her when the killer, Gerry, came on the line? Was she an accomplice or another hostage?

If she was an accomplice, why call the appeals line and state the killer's name in his presence? Surely, that would cause conflict between them? Deepa hadn't seen a second person, an accomplice, in the car when it passed us. Assuming that was the car, of course. So, had the accomplice stayed behind, then run off before the police turned up? Why would a deranged serial killer allow an accomplice who's trying to turn them both in to get away?

In that case, was the caller a second hostage who'd escaped? No, that didn't seem likely either. Annette had been bound and gagged and under the watchful eye of the killer. She couldn't escape. If the unknown woman had been a hostage too, how could she have freed herself from her bonds and gag and made a call on Annette's phone without Gerry noticing?

Torquemada purred in his sleep. I wanted to get a drink, but I didn't want to disturb him, so I stayed where I was and kept thinking.

Suppose the unknown woman had managed to do all that. Why would she disguise her voice? The killer took the phone from her. So, what happened to her after that? Surely the killer wouldn't have allowed her to escape and possibly call for help?

I frowned. The only thing that made sense to me was that there wasn't a second person, an unknown hostage who called the appeals line. There was only the killer. He had Annette in his car, bound and gagged. For some reason, he phoned the appeals line. Maybe because of guilt. Or shame. Or for a laugh.

But the original caller sounded like a woman. What was it she said? Something like 'I know the killer. His name's Gerry.'

I sat bolt upright on the sofa, dislodging Torquemada, who meowed in protest and resettled next to me.

Yes. That's it. The killer talked about themselves in the third person in a different voice. Sounded like a woman's voice, at first. Seconds later, it was a completely different personality. A different person, in the same body.

I pondered that for a while. The killer was crazy, sure, but this was a special kind of crazy. A kind I didn't readily have a name for, but some fancy psychiatrist would. There were few psychiatrists left in Quake City, and those who hadn't moved away to more stable areas after the earthquakes were doing a lucrative trade in private practice.

I needed a drink. Unwilling to clamber over Torquemada and risk disturbing him, I climbed over the back of the sofa. I kicked off my shoes—I shouldn't have had them on the sofa anyway—and went to the kitchen for a glass of water.

Gerry probably wasn't the killer's actual name. The sick individual killing people would have subconsciously invented him to blame for the murders that his—or maybe her—conscious mind could not cope with. In a moment of clarity, or of conscience, he or she tried to tell us, but that moment passed and Gerry took over.

I shuddered. How awful, to have your body hijacked by a separate violent identity.

But that raised more questions. A chicken and egg type question. Who's the "real" person? Gerry, or the unknown woman? Who's in primary control of that body? When did the second identity appear, or has it always been there, dormant?

Perhaps I needed something stronger than water to drink, but I didn't want to cloud my reasoning just yet. Later would do. I returned to the sofa and sat next to Torquemada. I thought hard. The cat just slept.

Such a person as this must have a history of mental health issues. I'd been right about that from the beginning. But it was possible—even likely—that this particular issue hadn't arisen before the earthquakes and was therefore undiagnosed. Something had recently triggered a crisis for them, and they were unable to deal with the repercussions of it. Instead, their subconscious mind had thrown up Gerry, who had his own way of dealing with things. Violently.

What was the crisis that caused this? What was the trigger for it? Something in the past that Deepa's been searching for? Or something in the present? If it was personal, there'd be no way we could know what it was.

My head was spinning, and it wasn't because of the water I'd been drinking. Contemplating the fractured mind of the Messenger Shooter was intense and complicated.

Did they know of each other, these distinct personalities? Yes, the caller referred to Gerry, and she said Gerry wasn't listening. But then she said Gerry *was* listening. And it was just after that when Gerry took over.

I rested my head in my hands, tired from trying to work all this out. So, the caller knew of Gerry, but it seemed that Gerry may not be aware of what the other identity was saying or doing at all times. Maybe Gerry was dormant and only took over in times of stress—and phoning the police appeals line to report an abduction would surely be one of those situations. But does the caller always know there's a hidden persona, Gerry, waiting to surface, or not? Perhaps not. Maybe it's the same both ways, they're only aware of each other when they're about to cross over.

Hell's teeth, this was hard to fathom. I'd get a complex myself trying to figure this mental mess out.

The door handle turned. Deepa came in carrying her laptop bag and containers of takeaway food. My stomach rumbled at the smell of the Thai curries. I'd fed Torquemada, but eaten nothing myself.

"Are you all right?" She put the takeaways on the coffee table and her laptop bag on the floor by the sofa. "You look dreadful."

"It's just this case getting me down. Thanks for bringing the food."

"It might not be hot. Your neighbour stopped me on the way in, and I had trouble getting away."

That didn't surprise me. I hadn't even heard the stairs creaking, I was so busy concentrating.

I fetched plates and cutlery, and we shared out the meal. It was delicious. Thank goodness she hadn't expected me to cook. Yet. For once, we didn't talk about the investigation while we ate. I appreciated that. It allowed the murky thoughts in my mind to clear.

After eating, though, I couldn't avoid it. "I should go back to the police station. Find out what else turned up on the appeals line."

"Can't it wait until morning?" Deepa evidently wasn't convinced that I'd learn anything. Or maybe she didn't want me to leave her alone in the apartment.

"Someone might have phoned up with information about the killer after we left."

"I'm sure Inspector O'Toole would have let you know by now if there was anything important. Besides, they're probably still fielding calls. It can wait. Let's go in early tomorrow."

I relented. "You're right, they'll still be getting calls and sifting through information. I've got something better for us to do."

"What's that?" Deepa raised an eyebrow.

"I've made a breakthrough on the killer's psychological profile. I want to talk it through with you. Maybe you can use that for your next article, get some money for us. Then I'll go through the police database again looking for any likely matches."

"Okay. That sounds good." She pulled her notebook and a pen out of her bag. "Go ahead."

"Give me a minute." I tidied up the remains of our meal, which, because we ate off paper plates with plastic cutlery, meant it all went into the bin. Even easier than a dishwasher. Then I told Deepa my theory about the killer's multiple personalities. She wrote fast, and she wrote a lot. I read it afterwards to see if I'd explained it fully. I had, but I still found it hard to believe.

Chapter 35

Day 7, morning

DEEPA EMERGED from my room at six thirty in the morning. "Rise and shine, sleepyhead. Early start, remember?"

I groaned, rubbed my eyes, then extricated myself from the sofa and Torquemada's still-sleeping form. I'd slept in my clothes again. Giving up my room to Deepa had downsides. If it had any upsides at all, they hadn't happened yet.

"I'll go shower."

On my return to the living room / office, Deepa had made coffee and toast. Okay, maybe there were some upsides. She brought dinner. And made breakfast.

We ate quickly and in silence, under a cloud of worry. I had to catch this killer before more people died. The police were getting nowhere—they'd even had to move the partition walls in their incident room to make room for all the victims' photos.

What was the killer doing at the moment while I munched on buttered toast and marmalade? Also eating toast? Cleaning the shotgun? Setting out for another murder?

"All right. Come on, then." Deepa stood and reached for her purple puffer jacket and laptop bag.

"You're coming with me?"

"Yep. I don't want you to leave me here by myself with that mad killer on the loose targeting media personalities and postal workers."

I quirked an eyebrow. "Are you a media personality now, Deepa?"

She pouted. "Not as such. But I have been writing about him, so, in his mind, perhaps I am. Who knows what someone like that really thinks? And if he reads the *Richter Mail,* he'll know about me—and you. I don't want to be alone anyplace he could track me down."

Mrs Werther's door opened a crack as we went past.

We hurried by.

§

The police station was less than five minutes from my apartment by car, but a police officer flagged us down half way there. I pulled over, cursing. It wasn't dawn yet, and the light from the crescent moon and stars was unable to penetrate the clouds. A light, steady rain fell. At least half the streetlights didn't work.

But one enthusiastic police officer for traffic revenue was working. The same one who fined me yesterday grinned when I lowered my window.

"You need to get that headlight fixed." He brought his digital fine generation gadget into view.

"Have you nothing better to do? You stopped me yesterday."

"You should have gotten it fixed. Go on. Off with you."

"You're letting me off with a warning?"

"No. I've got all your details from yesterday. It only took me a moment to issue a second fine."

I raised my window, grimacing.

Deepa stared daggers at him as we drove off. "What an asshole."

"The bastard was probably waiting for me. I'd better get it repaired, then." How I'd get around town I didn't know, but I couldn't afford the fines mounting up even more. The guy could meet his quota with my car alone, otherwise.

I drove to a mechanics' garage in one of Riverside's side streets. It was a place I vaguely trusted. I'd been there before and convinced them somehow that I knew something about cars other than how to drive them, so they wouldn't cheat me too much. Post-quake, most places weren't that honest—you'd go in for a replacement spark plug and they'd find numerous other things that needed replacing at the same time.

"Let's get something to eat and drink." Although we'd already eaten breakfast, I needed another coffee and time to think. We went into the Cupquake café. I ate and drank with gusto.

Deepa picked at the edges of her pastry and sipped her coffee. "I wonder if the killer is going to kill someone today." She gasped. "That sounded so... so mundane, like I was asking you if you thought it might rain."

Yeah. Terrible. Thinking of the murder forecast. Dull morning, eighty percent chance of homicide in the afternoon, unsettled tonight.

"Unfortunately, Deepa, nothing will stop this killer except us, Inspector O'Toole, or an Act of God. And I don't think we can put much faith in the latter two."

She nibbled at her croissant. Would she let me eat it if she didn't want it?

"You think I've been wasting my time at the news archives—"

"No." I shook my head, trying to stop 'yes' bouncing around inside it. "You might uncover something."

"I'll give it another two or three hours, and if I find nothing, I'm done with it. The trouble is, I don't know what else I can do. I don't know how to track down criminals."

And you probably think I don't know how to either. I frowned. Was I thinking that about Deepa, or myself? Or both of us?

We'd got nowhere. The killer kept slaughtering people, apparently at random, and it was getting worse. More vicious. What would stop them? Would they tire of it? Move to Australia and take their bloodthirsty hobby with them? Or be caught by pure rotten luck?

"What are you thinking, Danny?"

"I thinking I'm not hungry anymore."

§

Inspector O'Toole and Sergeant Ling weren't in the station yet. Early morning sunlight filtered through the blinds. Deepa and I made our way to the incident room where we had taken the appeals line calls. Peter was the only one there.

"You haven't been here all night, have you, Pete?"

"Actually, I have, Danny." Peter yawned. "The calls slowed down after you took off last night, though. I heard what happened. Awful. When are we going to get this guy, do you think?"

"Soon. Very soon." I hoped. "I'd like to see the transcripts, please."

"No problem. We caught up on that in the early hours of the morning. There's been nothing much since then."

I sat at a nearby desk. Deepa dragged a chair over and sat next to me, her notebook out. She never goes anywhere without a notebook, it seems. Peter put a pile of printouts on the desk.

"Thanks, Pete. Why don't you go home now? We'll field any calls that come in until someone else arrives."

"Nice one, Danny." He grabbed his jacket and left.

"That was helpful, but what if we need to leave before then?"

"It'll be okay. I'm sure other constables will be in soon. Remember, I work closely with the police at times. It pays to be nice to everyone. In this town, you never know when a constable will be promoted to sergeant, or a sergeant to inspector."

"So, you sensibly want to keep them all onside." Deepa smiled.

"Yes… but I'm also a helpful guy."

She chuckled. "Let's look over these transcripts together, then. After that, I'll go to the news archives—for the last time."

"Okay." I started leafing through the call transcripts.

We came across the transcript of the killer's phone call, and I pulled it aside. "You can't tell from this transcript, but it sounded like two distinct people. The first, a woman, said the killer's name was Gerry—but I believe that's a fake name. The second voice, Gerry, was distinctly different from the first."

"But you believe they're the same person, right?" Deepa looked unsure. Her head wobbled from side to side.

"I know it sounds farfetched, but the person we're looking for isn't like you or I or any typical person. We'll listen to the call later. You'll see what I mean."

"All right. After we've been through the rest of the transcripts."

On we went, wading through pages of prank calls, false accusations, false witnesses, false confessions. Detectives had marked them as questionable at some point during the night, either after speaking to the individual named, or to the caller, in detail.

Deepa dropped another transcript on our discard pile. "Why are we wasting our time on these? They've all been closed."

"Because sometimes detectives take shortcuts. They don't investigate the call, they simply mark it as false and close it, because to them it sounded like a prank call. Why waste police resources chasing it up, then? That's their thinking, anyway."

"But what if they're wrong?"

"Then the killer slips through the net until the next time."

Deepa shuddered.

"See this one." I pointed at the page. "Someone named Jake Munro as a possibility, but the constable marked it as an unreliable caller and closed it. I interviewed Jake Munro the other day. He's a small-time drug dealer and conman with a conviction for assault. I'd like to know why the constable thought the caller was unreliable. We can't tell from the transcript."

Deepa noted the caller's name and number. "All right, we can check them out later."

"We should listen to the call for any inflections in the caller's voice that might tell us something. Obviously, they're not on the transcript."

"Sure thing."

We looked further. More prank calls. Then something useful—another witness for the car racing from one of the early crime scenes, describing it as a navy-blue station wagon. That made two callers confirming the same description for the car. Shame they didn't get the number plate.

A few minutes later, another name grabbed my attention: Linda McKenzie. The caller hadn't given their name or number. The constable who took the call had marked it as 'CPC'—crazy person calling.

Interesting. I blinked. "I interviewed her, too. She'd been hospitalised for aggressive behaviour due to a mental health issue a few years ago. She didn't seem dangerous when I spoke to her."

"And as the call was anonymous, we can't ask the caller for any actual details of why they named her."

"No. There are no details here at all." Odd? Maybe not. Sometimes, people just don't want to get involved. "We should listen to that call, too. See if we pick up anything from the caller's tone of voice."

"Sure."

We went through the remaining transcripts in half an hour. There wasn't anything useful. Someone blamed aliens. Someone else blamed vampires. I'd never heard of shotgun-wielding vampires. The North Koreans got another mention, though that might have been the same caller phoning back to get his kicks again.

"Okay, let's listen to the calls we picked out." Now we would hear the callers' inflections and tone.

A few constables and detectives were in the office now. One or two of them looked our way twice, maybe wondering what we were doing so early, or if we'd found something.

I asked one of them to give us access to the audio of the calls, starting with the one from the killer.

Deepa listened intently, not even making notes or saying a word, right through to the end. "I want to hear that again."

I didn't. It sent shivers down my spine. But I replayed it for her anyway.

She listened just as carefully the second time. "I see what you mean. At first, it sounds like it's two distinct people, but there's something about it—though the voice is very different—that made me sense it was the same person."

"Yes, but I can't explain what it is that gave me that impression." I scratched my head under my fedora.

"I think I know. The caller's breathing sounded exactly the same for both voices."

"Their breathing? Are you being serious?"

Deepa inclined her head. "I'm just explaining why I felt it was the same person speaking."

"Okay. You might be right. When the caller or callers weren't talking, the breathing sounded similar, but it could have been a coincidence."

"I thought you don't believe in coincidences."

She had me there.

Deepa continued. "If that wasn't the reason you thought it was the same person, then what was it?"

"I told you last night. It was the logical impracticality of the situation if there'd been a second person there, plus Annette Graves."

She smiled broadly, and all my morning grumpiness melted like butter on a fresh hotcake. "We have different methods, you and I. That's why we're such an awesome team." She punched me on the arm playfully, and I pretended it hurt to make her laugh.

Debbie called out from her desk. "You guys all right over there? You want to get a room or something?"

The heat rose up my face like a flash of lightning. Deepa turned away, fiddling with her laptop bag, her face impassive. I turned too, feeling foolish. On the other side of the room, a couple of constables laughed, but at what, I wasn't sure. I didn't look up.

"Come on." I turned back to the screen. In my head, I said, 'Let's get some hotcakes for breakfast', but what came out of my mouth was: "Let's listen to the other calls."

We listened to the call in which someone named Jake Munro as a suspect. The caller was adamant that Jake was the devil incarnate. We'd already picked that up from the transcript. But what hadn't shown up on the transcript was that the caller was drunk, on drugs, or both, and giggling permeated the background.

"Prank call." I crossed it off our list.

"Can you be sure?"

"Yeah. We can come back to it if there's nothing else to follow up on, but yeah, I'm sure this one is a waste of time. The caller should be charged." I made a note about it and shoved it over to Peter's desk.

"One to go, then."

The anonymous one naming Linda McKenzie as the killer. Probably another prank call, like most of them on the night. But I played the audio anyway.

Chapter 36

"I DON'T WANT to leave my name." The caller was a woman, her voice muffled, unsteady because of age or nerves.

The constable's voice came on, calm and confident. "That's okay. Calls can be anonymous. Please tell me your information."

"I listened to the appeal on the television. I want to give you the name of the person who committed these crimes."

Pause. "Go ahead, I'm listening."

"First, I want you to understand that she is extremely dangerous. When you find her, she should be shot on sight, otherwise she will kill police officers and any innocent bystanders."

"Please give me the person's name, madam."

"I will." Tea cups rattled in the background, and a cuckoo clock sounded the half-hour. "I just want to make sure you know she is dangerous and you should not try to take her alive."

"Thank you, madam, I've noted your views about that. What is the name?"

"Linda McKenzie." The caller disconnected.

I checked the call log. "They couldn't fully trace the call. It originated from one of the southern suburbs, but that's all we know."

"She sure was adamant that this McKenzie woman be shot on sight. Isn't that unusual? Illegal, even, if she's not armed at the time?"

"Yes, it is. Maybe the constable was right not to investigate further. It could be a crazy neighbour or relative with some perceived grudge to bear. But I want to talk to Linda McKenzie again, because she was on my shortlist."

"You won't shoot her on sight, will you?"

I gave Deepa a sharp look. She smiled wryly.

"I think we're done here." I stood. "I'm going to go and get my car. It should be repaired by now."

"Okay. I'll walk back to your place to get my scooter, then I'll go to the news archives. Last time, I promise."

I chuckled. "You're addicted to the place."

"I'll phone you if I find something." She didn't look hopeful.

We left the police station and parted ways.

I strolled back to the mechanics' garage where I'd left my car. I couldn't pay for the repair yet, but I hadn't told them that when I left the car there. Maybe it had slipped my mind. I'd say that, anyway. The truth was I needed my share of the payments from Deepa's articles to pay for it, and we hadn't received anything yet. I hoped they'd give me a line of credit.

Colin, the owner, met me at the entrance. He wiped his greasy hands on the oily overalls he wore, then ruffled what was left of his hair.

"Danny, your car's buggered, mate."

"What? It's just the headlight, isn't it?" I leaned over to look past him. Part of what might have been my car lay in pieces on the workshop floor.

"Yeah, well, actually it isn't, mate. The slug you told us to look for must have ricocheted around the engine block and caused a lot of damage. It nicked a couple of lines, so the vehicle's been leaking fluids. The brakes were going to fail at any moment. There's little oil and water left due to the holes, and the slug smashed up the electronics and the—"

"Okay, okay. I don't want all the details, Colin. Just tell me when you can have it fixed by, and what it'll cost." Better not ask for the credit line just yet.

"That's just it, Danny. It's not worth repairing, mate. It'd be cheaper for you to get another car. Phone your insurance company."

I groaned. There was no way I would get the money from the tight-fisted insurance company without a fight. They were too over-burdened with all the earthquake claims they were trying to turn down. By the time they got to my claim, there'd be no money left anyway. They'd probably say the damage to the car was due to the proverbial "Act of God". The devil, more like. Though neither of those deities happened to be the shooter.

"Sorry, mate, it's a tough break, but in good conscience I couldn't let you drive that car out of here. It's a death trap."

"That's thoughtful of you, Colin." He valued repeat business.

The mechanic stroked his chin. "Tell you what, I can use some of it for spare parts. I can give you two hundred bucks. That might tide you over until you get the insurance money." His voice trailed off. He knew as well as I did that I'd be more likely to get money out of the Mafia than the insurance company.

"All right." Two hundred dollars was better than nothing, right? When I needed to dash off to a crime scene, I could spend some of it on an Uber or a bus.

I collected the money, stuffed it in my pocket and strode home. The cool mid-morning air cleared my head. There were upsides to having my car ruined. I was being too bleak about the insurance money. Surely, with a well-placed suggestion that they pay up (or else), I'd get the insurance pay-out. And I hoped that snotty cop who'd fined me twice for the broken headlight would be pointlessly waiting in his car late at night and early in the morning, hoping to snaffle me again.

I reached my apartment building and climbed the stairs, wearied from the burden of trying to identify the killer, find evidence that would satisfy Inspector O'Toole and a jury, and catch them. The public appeal may have thrown up some leads. Or maybe just more red herrings.

The stair near the top creaked beneath my feet as usual. I didn't mind that—it meant that no one could sneak up and surprise me in my apartment. Unfortunately, it also alerted Mrs Werther.

But this time it didn't. Odd. The door to her apartment was open. She must have heard. She wouldn't have gone out and left the door open, would she?

I almost walked past. It's seldom that I'm quick enough to slip by before she corners me and quizzes me on my business, who I've been with that day, or told me about her various ailments and hypochondriacal complaints.

Something was wrong. It was too quiet, for a start.

I sniffed. A metallic smell lingered in the air.

Chapter 37

I PAUSED, LISTENING. Still nothing. I brushed my coat pocket, feeling for my Glock 17 handgun. It wasn't there. I'd left it in my apartment. I'd have to start taking it with me. Too late this time.

I edged along the landing, my heartbeat pounding in my eardrums, dread pitting my stomach. Had the killer been here? Was Mrs Werther lying inside, lifeless, the latest victim? Was the perp still in there, waiting for me?

Walking past the doorway would be too dangerous. I'd be an open target. Instead, I peeked around the edge. Mrs Werther's slippered toes pointed towards the ceiling.

Time to be bold. I shoved the door open as hard as I could. It crashed into the wall. I dived inside and rolled on the polished wooden floorboards, rising to a crouch.

No one there. I stood and crossed to the kitchen doorway, grabbing a lamp as a makeshift weapon as I went by. The plug pinged out of the wall socket.

The kitchen was empty too. I checked the bedroom, then the bathroom. No one there.

I let out the breath I'd been holding and put the lamp on the table. In the distance, sirens blared. The police were coming. Someone must have reported hearing the shot.

I knelt by Mrs Werther. She'd been shot in the chest at close range. Probably at the doorway, and the blast threw her back into her room. Blood pooled and seeped into the flowery carpet. Her eyes stared at the ceiling, a look of shock on her face as if she saw something up there that didn't meet her approval.

But she saw nothing at all.

A stabbing pain swept through my chest. Guilt pangs swallowed me. I felt weak and dry-retched. Mrs Werther would still be alive if I wasn't working on this case. She died because the killer came looking for me.

The door downstairs crashed open. Several pairs of booted feet rushed inside.

I called out. "Up here. First apartment on your right at the top of the stairs."

They came up, armed, armoured, ready for anything. Two of them flashed past, racing towards my apartment. Another pair entered Mrs Werther's apartment, guns levelled, looking everywhere. One of them went to check the other rooms, while the other fixed his weapon on me.

Inspector O'Toole, trailed by Amy Ling, followed them into the room. "Relax, Jones. He's with us." The officer lowered his weapon.

"I came home and found my neighbour dead. I've looked around, but there's no one here."

The inspector cocked his head. "Checked on your place?"

"Not yet. I saw my neighbour's door open, and her lying on the floor like this. I didn't get as far as my apartment."

A shout came from down the hall. "All clear."

That meant my apartment and the empty one beside it. The killer had gone. I got to my feet. There was nothing I could do for Mrs Werther now. I needed to check my own place. Was Torquemada safe?

I brushed past O'Toole and onto the landing. The armed officers were on their way out. The coroner was coming up the stairs. I hurried on to my apartment, Amy Ling tagging along behind.

Someone had ransacked my office. My living area.

I looked around. No sign of the cat. I called out. "Torquemada."

"What?" Amy spun to face me.

"My cat." I peered behind the sofa. Not there. My stomach churned for a moment, before a tentative meow came from the top of one of the bookcases. Torquemada peeped over the edge.

I sighed in relief.

"Are you all right?" Amy stepped closer. "After finding your neighbour dead, I mean?"

"No, I feel awful." My insides quivered.

"Have a look around. Take your time. Tell me if anything's missing."

I did a quick inventory. My laptop was still there. "The papers scattered on the desk weren't like that before—the intruder's done that. I'd have to go through them to see if they've taken anything, but it doesn't look like—wait, what's this?" I indicated a sheet of paper lying on the chair behind the desk.

"Don't touch it. We'll dust it for fingerprints." Amy pulled out her phone and took a photo.

On the paper was a hand-written message in red ink. The writing was rough, even childish in its form, but the meaning was clear:

I had to do it. He got what he deserved, the fucking bastard.

Stop investigating. The police too. Stop investigating, and I stop killing.

You don't stop, and I kill someone every day. One person a day.

What do I care?

Blood smudged the bottom of the page, below the writing, like an illegible signature, signing off on his crimes.

"This note must refer to one of the male victims. Who, though?"

Bile rose in my throat. The perp had killed Mrs Werther for what? Because she came out of her apartment to say hello, thinking it was me on the landing? So he could leave a *note*?

I swallowed, driving the bile down, and gritted my teeth. Now it was personal. I'd find this monster and bring them to justice.

O'Toole entered the room. "A woman in the house next door called 111 and reported what she thought sounded like a gunshot. I spoke to her just now. She saw a station wagon parked outside, but it was gone when she'd finished making the phone call. It all happened about fifteen minutes ago. We have patrols out looking for the car, but it looks like the killer's gotten away. The description's too vague to find them anyway."

I studied the inspector. He was fiddling with his phone. Should I tell him my multiple personality theory? No, not yet. I'd make sure of it myself first.

"I can't see anything missing." I ducked down behind the desk. Papers were strewn on the floor, but I was looking for my Glock 17 handgun. It was in a secret compartment on the underside of the desk where I'd left it. Beside it was the shotgun I'd taken from the Gruesome Crew. Now, *that's* more like it. I pulled the shotgun out of its hiding place and covertly slipped it into a deep inside pocket of my raincoat.

I gave a full statement to a constable while O'Toole, Amy Ling and a group of SOCOs looked around both apartments for evidence and clues. They needn't have bothered. The killer had come only to leave a message, not to rob me. Mrs Werther was an incidental hindrance. All the perp had left behind, apart from the message, was a shotgun cartridge.

Chapter 38

Day 7, afternoon

I LEFT THE POLICE to conclude their search at my apartment. Out on the footpath, I felt the pocket with my wallet. It bulged with the two hundred dollars, because Colin had paid me in ten-dollar notes from his petty change jar.

Then I called Deepa. She answered on the second ring.

"Danny, I have news."

"Me too, and it's bad."

Pause. "You go first."

I told her, my hand gripping my phone with whitened knuckles as I imagined Deepa tensing when I described finding Mrs Werther shot dead and a note on my chair.

"So, the Messenger Shooter leaves a message. What irony."

"The perp wouldn't see it that way. They're getting more desperate, more dangerous, Deepa."

"Don't blame yourself for not being there, Danny."

"I just want to nail that monster."

"Let me tell you what I found."

"Go ahead." I started walking through the steady rain towards the coffee shop, pulling my raincoat around me. A coffee would help clear my head, allow me to focus and work out what I needed to do.

"I read an old article about Chris Dodd. Seven years ago, a dog bit him when he was delivering the post. The bite needed twenty stitches. He reported it, and the dog had to be put down."

Chris Dodd? The second victim? "That's interesting, Deepa. Did you get an address?"

"Yep. It's outside the city limits, west of Fallswell. The news report didn't say who lived there, though."

"We can try to find out. Remember the perp killed Chris Dodd's dog, even though it was secured in a dog run? Surely that's not a coincidence."

"Exactly. That's why I thought it was important. Maybe it was for revenge. Though why the killer waited seven years, I don't know."

"Maybe he or she was in prison. Or in a psych ward. Maybe they didn't know how to find Dodd. Or maybe they tried to put it behind themselves, until recently, when something triggered the first of the psychotic episodes and the violent second personality came forth."

"That makes sense. But if Chris Dodd was the primary target, why did the perp kill Ricky Cohen first? And everyone else?"

I grimaced, not that Deepa could see that. "The killer is crazy and ruthless. Maybe Ricky Cohen was a warm-up for the main event and killing others is to divert us from the actual target."

"That's sick."

"Well, yes. Or it could be that they killed Ricky Cohen accidentally. Remember he and Chris Dodd had just switched postal routes that day."

"So, Ricky Cohen's death might be merely because of mistaken identity?"

"Yes, it's possible." Something about that gnawed at the back of my mind. There was more to it, but what? I needed time to think.

"And the others?"

"Now the perp's addicted to killing and probably can't control themselves. The violent second personality, Gerry, I mean."

"I'm finished at the archives. I'll come over. Where are you?"

"The Cupquake Café." I'd just arrived, and I pulled open the door. "Can you meet me there with your laptop? My apartment is part of the crime scene and the police wouldn't let me take mine."

"See you in five minutes." She disconnected.

I went inside, ordered two coffees, and sat in a window booth so I could keep a lookout for Deepa. The drinks arrived moments before she did.

"Get your car repaired okay?"

I shook my head. "The car's scrap. The slug did a lot more damage than we thought."

"Sorry to hear that, Danny."

"Yeah. I liked that car. I didn't want to have to replace it." What I meant was I couldn't afford to. "Anyway, the police will have my apartment cordoned off for hours, so we'll have to use your laptop to access their databases. We need to find out who owned that place outside Fallswell where Chris Dodd was attacked by the dog, then track them down."

"Have you told Inspector O'Toole about it?"

"Not yet."

Deepa looked away. "We're handling this on our own then, are we?"

"For now." For good, in fact. The killer had made this personal.

"Danny, we can't do everything on our own."

"Yes, we can. We must. I won't leave it up to O'Toole. He's always two steps behind."

"And we're only one step behind, is that it?" Deepa sighed. "At least I've got fresh material for an article."

"Speaking of that, is the *Richter Mail* going to pay out soon for what we've done so far?" I stressed the 'we'.

"In the next couple of weeks, I suppose, but it won't be enough for you to buy a new car, if that's what you're thinking."

"Of course not." I frowned. What now? A private investigator needs a vehicle. I must work something out soon.

Deepa drained her coffee, put the cup down and unzipped her bag. "Tell me how you've got access to the police databases." She pulled out her laptop and put it on the table in front of me.

"A well-placed bribe to one of their IT staff who set me up with a fake account. Since the earthquakes, everything's changed. They're not so tight on their network security anymore. Too much else for them to do and not enough budget, I suppose."

"I guess you don't want me to write an article about that."

I glowered. "No, I don't."

"Relax, I was just kidding."

"All right. Let's get to work." I logged into the main police system. From there, I could jump to all other government databases. It was better, quicker and safer than tracking people down and needling them for information.

"What are you going to do?"

"There must be a police report for the dog bite, if the court ordered the dog to be destroyed. Do you have a date?"

"Yep, here." Deepa passed me her phone with the Notes app open where she'd noted details of the incident. "Do you think we're onto something with this, Danny? Do you really think the killer is taking revenge for their dead dog by killing the postman who had it put down seven years ago? It seems such a weak motive. And what about all the other victims?"

That's true—normal people wouldn't do that. But the killer wasn't a typical person. "I think the killer's evil identity—Gerry—was triggered by something, but we don't know what. He's been dormant all this time. To him, the death of the dog might be a lot more personal and feel like it was mere days ago."

Deepa nodded. "Okay. I don't understand this psychological stuff, but I'll take your word for it." She shuffled closer to me, brushing my thigh, or, rather, closer to the laptop.

It took only a few minutes to find the report of the dog bite. "A couple, Ben Miller and Bronwyn Lewis, rented the place. Let's see what we can find on them. It'll take only a few minutes."

Deepa picked up her phone and tapped a few keys. "Ben Miller, labourer, committed suicide six years ago. So, he's not the killer." She tapped her phone some more.

Her swift research stunned me. "How did you find that out so quickly?"

"Births, deaths and marriages, online, premium access. I use it a lot for work."

"You're quicker than I am."

"Yes, we make an excellent team, like I said. I'm good with technology. You're good at… the stuff you do. Right, Bronwyn Lewis… oh, you're not going to believe this."

"What?" I craned my neck, trying to see her phone.

"Bronwyn Lewis is now Bronwyn Dodd. Chris Dodd's wife. They married three years ago."

My mind swirled like a mini tornado. "I didn't see that coming."

"Who could? Clearly, the dog didn't matter to her, or she forgave Chris for having it put down."

Thoughts rattled through my head like an old train on wooden tracks. "It's possible Ben Miller killed himself after his partner left him for Chris Dodd."

"That's speculation. We can't know that for sure."

"We should go talk to her, see what she has to say about it."

Deepa inclined her head. "Are you thinking she might have had her husband killed while she was overseas?"

"Can't rule it out, can we?"

"But it's so farfetched. You're thinking she left her partner, married the guy who had her dog put down, then hired a hitman years later to take revenge while she went overseas to give herself an alibi? That's unbelievable."

"Yes, it is. That's not what I'm thinking. It seems too much of a coincidence, that's all, and I don't believe in coincidences." I sat back on the bench seat. "We must be missing a big piece of the puzzle."

"What is it?"

I shook my head. "I don't know yet. Let's talk to Bronwyn Dodd. Maybe we'll find out."

Deepa's brow creased. "She came back when the police told her about her husband, right? Why haven't we questioned her before?"

"Lack of time, Deepa. Since the third murder, we've either been at crime scenes or trying to profile the killer and determine likely matches. I didn't think we'd learn much more from the relatives, actually. Though it sounds like Bronwyn Dodd might be a different matter."

Deepa grabbed her laptop and slipped it into her bag. "Let's go."

We went outside into the brisk morning air, the sun dim through silvery cloud. I shivered. My neighbour murdered. A killer on the loose. A police inspector who thinks he's chasing six different serial killers and has no idea where to begin. And me, without any wheels.

Should I get a taxi?

Deepa put on her motorcycle helmet. She tossed her head. "What are you waiting for? Get on."

I didn't have a helmet, but what the hell. I sat awkwardly, unsure what to do with my hands. What should I hold on to? There are no handlebars for a pillion passenger.

Deepa revved the scooter's engine. Now that I was sitting atop the thing, it sounded less like a hairdryer and more like a roaring mechanical beast. Though that might have been my imagination running wild.

We started moving, and I gripped Deepa around the waist, shuffling as close as I could. This wasn't bad. I could get used to this. Very comfortable.

She sped up, arcing the scooter to the right across the road, around the corner on a late orange light and down Crumblo Street. My hair streamed behind me, and I realised, too late, that my hat had flown off behind us. I glanced backward, only to see it being run over by a car and squashed flat.

Deepa shouted so I would hear her over the wind. "Stay still."

I looked forward again, over her shoulder. Shops and houses whizzed by. It felt like we were powering along well above the speed limit. My heart raced. I felt exposed on the scooter compared to the relative safety of a car.

Twenty minutes later, we arrived at the Dodds' house. I'd begun to enjoy the ride, and not just because I had my arms around Deepa. No, I mustn't follow that line of thought. Not at the moment. We had a killer to catch.

Deepa parked the scooter on the side of the road, and we dismounted. She removed her helmet. "How was the ride?"

"Cool. It was so fast."

"Yep, it's 200cc, not one of those little 50cc putt-putts."

"Ah. You need a motorcycle license for that, don't you?"

"Do you? I've never thought about it."

Okay. No license, then.

"Your hat's gone."

"Forget about it. Let's see if Bronwyn Dodd is home."

We approached the front door. The police had finished and removed the crime scene tapes, cleaned up the blood and taken away the dead dog. We knocked on the door.

Moments later, Bronwyn answered. I guess she was on bereavement leave from her work. When we introduced ourselves as working with the police, she let us in. We followed her to the kitchen. She sat at the table where, only a few days ago, the perp had murdered her husband.

Chapter 39

"WHATEVER IT IS you want, make it quick. I've got a bloody funeral to arrange."

Bronwyn Dodd's vitriolic remark caught me by surprise. Deepa, though, kept her cool. "How are you holding up after your husband's murder?"

"Oh, don't worry about me. No one ever does. I can look after myself."

"Can you think of anyone who might have wanted to kill your husband?" I knew the police would already have asked this, but I wanted to get myself into the conversation.

"No. He wouldn't have said 'boo' to a goose, that man. And I've already told the coppers all that. Why are you here asking the same bloody questions?"

"We understand you're angry—" Deepa's attempt to console Bronwyn didn't get far.

"Of course I'm bloody angry. Think I can afford the funeral costs? Look at this place. Does it look like I live in the lap of luxury here? And now it'll be twice as hard to get by."

Deepa cast me a despairing glance. Bronwyn was a distressed, angry, spiteful, or simply unpleasant woman. Or all of those. She didn't appear to care much for her husband either—I remembered no wedding photos were hanging on the walls or sitting on shelves anywhere.

I tried again. "Okay, we don't want to take up much of your time—"

"Good. Get on with it, then."

"About seven years ago, you lived in a place outside Fallswell with your previous partner, correct?"

Bronwyn's eyes narrowed. "That's right. What about it?"

"At that time, your dog bit a postman, and the dog was put down after the postman, now your late husband, filed a complaint."

"I don't bloody believe this. My husband's been murdered, and you're chasing up about a dog bite years ago. What the hell?"

Her fierce glare almost knocked me over. I raised a hand in an effort to get her to calm down. I didn't think it would work, but it would give me some protection if she threw something at me.

"I'm only trying to understand the big picture. When did your relationship with Chris start? Was it before or after the dog was put down?"

"You mean, was I screwing him while I was still with my previous partner. Yes, I was. What of it?"

Deepa's eyes narrowed. "And your previous partner, Ben Miller, killed himself a few months later?"

"I think so. Maybe."

"You *think* so?"

"I didn't see him again after I left. Why are you two here? Why the hell are you asking me these things? It's all old history. Who cares about it?"

There must be more to this. We were missing something. "I'm interested in the dog. If you were already in a relationship with Chris Dodd, why did he have your dog put down? Wouldn't he have been more forgiving? You said, quote, 'he wouldn't say boo to a goose', unquote."

"It wasn't up to him. It was the rules. Any postman gets badly bitten and the manager writes up a complaint for the coppers. Chris had to sign it, that's all."

This wasn't making sense. The killer had targeted Chris in his home—this house—and deliberately killed the dog in the back yard. The dog that was tied up and posed no threat. Was the dog part of the motive, or not? If not, why kill it? Out of spite? Or maybe…

"Who did the dog belong to at your old place?"

"My daughter. It was her dog. I didn't even like the bloody thing." Bronwyn scowled.

I glanced at Deepa. Her mouth opened in surprise. This was news.

"How old is your daughter?" My throat rasped the question.

"She's twenty-three, I think. Or it might be twenty-two. I haven't seen her since I left Ben. Good riddance, I say. She was always a bloody disappointment."

A chill ran through me. This woman had a heart of stone. If there was a heart there at all. She'd abandoned her daughter and partner without so much as a backward glance, and she didn't seem to care much about her husband's murder.

Deepa tilted her head and wobbled it, as was her custom. "So, you don't remember exactly how old your daughter is? Do you remember if she was upset when her dog was put down?"

"Oh, for sure, she was. I didn't hear the end of it for days. Crying, shrieking, whining, the lot. Even a cuff around the ear wouldn't stop her squawking." She chuckled. "You know, the funny thing was, even though I told her it wasn't Chris' doing, she blamed him for everything. The dog and more besides, lots of rubbish that she made up."

"And why was that funny?" I kept my voice as level as I could, but bitterness still coated my voice. Bronwyn Dodd was a deplorable woman.

"Because for everything else she did wrong, she'd blame her friend Gerry, and that was bloody ridiculous, because Gerry didn't even exist. He was just an imaginary friend she pretended she had."

Gerry. The evil second personality of the killer. Deepa and I swapped glances.

Deepa took a sharp intake of breath. "What's your daughter's name?" Her lips mouthed the words 'if you can remember'.

"Linda. Bloody loser Linda."

"Linda Lewis? Linda Miller?"

"No, Ben wasn't her father. I had her before I met him. She had her father's surname. McKenzie." She snorted. "Another asshole I haven't seen for years."

Linda McKenzie. The clock repairer who I'd interviewed days before. She'd seemed like a normal woman who'd got on top of her mental illness, started a small business and got on with life. I hadn't seen the evil that lurked beneath the surface. But how could I? I wasn't sure that Linda knew much about that side of herself either.

"We'll leave you in peace, Bronwyn. Try to… take it easy."

She snarled at us. "That's not going to happen, is it?"

We left as quickly as we could. I felt disconcerted all the way out to the street, as if her fierce gaze could drill a hole in my back.

"What a nasty bitch." Deepa was understating it.

"I ought to phone the inspector, let him know what we've found out." Not that I wanted to, as I wanted to solve the case myself, but I felt obligated.

I pulled out my cheap phone, dialled and put the call on speakerphone. O'Toole answered after the first ring. "Inspector, Deepa and I interviewed Bronwyn Dodd. The killer is her daughter, a woman named Linda McKenzie. Here's her address." I reeled it off. "You should take her in for questioning."

"Are you sure, Ashford? Amy and I interviewed Bronwyn Dodd after she returned from Australia, and nothing came to light."

"It's definitely Linda McKenzie, Inspector. She has a mental illness of some kind, I don't know what, but she's not in complete control of herself at all times. McKenzie's the serial killer. She killed them all, I'm sure of it."

"All of them? But what about the different M.O.s?"

"Inspector, trust me. Just bring her in."

"On it. I'll despatch a squad to pick her up."

I breathed a sigh of relief now that O'Toole was listening. "I'll come to the station to help interview her." I paused. "That's if you want me to."

"Sure, why not?" The inspector disconnected.

Deepa pressed the starter button on her Vespa. "Get on. Let's motor."

I slid behind her. The return ride was just as thrilling as the first. I could get used to this. I clung onto Deepa as she skilfully navigated around various potholes and abandoned roadworks on the way to the Riverside police station.

The novelty of the scooter ride faded after a short while as my mind started churning. Linda McKenzie was the killer, all right. But what had triggered her after all this time? And something else tickled the back of my mind… Abruptly, I realised what it was. The caller on the appeals line who had named Linda McKenzie. She was right about that. Was it a guess, or did she know more? And why had she insisted that Linda be shot on sight?

Chapter 40

DEEPA STOPPED OUTSIDE the police station, squeezing into a tiny gap between parked cars, an advantage of a scooter I hadn't considered before. If my car had still been drivable, I would've had to park it two- or three-minutes' walk away.

Two patrol cars and a van drove out of the police parking lot and passed us.

I let go of Deepa's waist and slid off the scooter while the engine was still purring. Deepa didn't switch it off.

"What are you doing?" I wanted to get inside and talk to O'Toole before the constables brought McKenzie in, but Deepa wasn't about to join me.

"I'm going to follow them." She nodded towards the police vehicles waiting at the nearest traffic lights.

"No. Wait, no, that might be dangerous."

Most of my words were drowned out as she revved the engine. "Can't hear you." The scooter kicked into motion, zipping out behind the police cars as the light turned green. I watched them disappear down Crumblo Street, Deepa keeping pace.

I should have gone with her. I'd been so fixated on getting to the station to talk with O'Toole about strategies for interviewing McKenzie that I hadn't given any thought about what Deepa might do. And what she would do, of course, was follow the story. She wanted to be present when the police arrested the Messenger Shooter.

That would get her the front-page exclusive feature in the *Richter Mail* that she so eagerly wanted, and a huge pay check for us both.

And I'd left her to go into the lion's den alone.

Well, not alone, exactly. There were a dozen police officers accompanying her. But she was going without me.

So, I was the one who was alone.

I climbed the steps and went inside, grinding my teeth, exasperated at my lack of foresight. Call myself a private investigator? I couldn't even detect that my partner was determined to see the capture of the killer we'd spent days hunting. Instead, I was cooling my heels at the police station, waiting for her to return. I couldn't even follow her, now that my car was kaput. If I called a taxi or waited for an occasional bus, the suspect capture would be over before I got there.

Unless McKenzie wasn't at home. That would give me a chance to catch up with Deepa. In that case, maybe I could persuade O'Toole that we should go looking for McKenzie, and we could discuss interview strategies on the way.

Yes, that would work. I took the stairs two at a time up to Inspector O'Toole's office.

Chapter 41

COPS LOOKING FOR ME. How do they know to come to my house? Did she *fucking tell them?*

No. I'd know if she'd done that. No, it wasn't her.

Then who was it?

Forget that. Can they see me parked down the road, in the shadows of the oak tree? Yeah, probably. Shit. Better get ready to move.

Ha ha, they're not even looking. They're running up the driveway. All of them.

They won't find me. I'm going to get the fuck out of here.

No, wait. Who's that on the scooter? She's not a cop.

I don't bloody believe it. It's that bitch who writes that shit about me in the paper.

What did she call me? 'The Messenger Shooter', wasn't it? What a fucking dumb name.

Hey.

She's a messenger.

Chapter 42

I LEANED FORWARD as O'Toole jabbed a button to put the phone on speaker. Hopefully, this was one of the officers reporting they had Linda McKenzie in custody. A crackling voice issued forth. "It's Sam. We haven't got her. She's not here."

"Is there a navy-blue station wagon on the premises?"

"No."

The inspector spoke up. "Thanks, Sam. Good work. Round everyone up and start looking in nearby areas, especially the shops. She might have gone out for an errand or for a coffee or something. I'll text you the number plate of her car. Pass it on."

"Will do, Inspector."

O'Toole disconnected the call. "Sam's clever. I'll have him up for promotion to Detective Sergeant after this. Or Debbie. Amy's leaving."

Most people leave this godforsaken ruined city if they have the chance. She probably had a job offer from one of the other police forces in the country.

"So, now we just wait." O'Toole tapped his fingers on the desk.

"I think we should go to the house ourselves. Sam and the others may have missed something that we might see." That *I* might see.

"Why don't you go by yourself, Ashford? I'm needed here to coordinate my team."

I fumed. I knew this might happen. My skin prickled. Something wasn't right. I picked up my phone and dialled Deepa.

No answer.

That didn't mean anything. She could be riding her scooter, unable to pick up the phone.

But why hadn't she called me from McKenzie's house? She'd know that I was at the station waiting to interview a suspect who hadn't been caught. We could have met up again.

I had a bad feeling about this.

"Inspector, could one of the constables give me a lift to McKenzie's house, please?"

"Give you a lift? We're the police, not a taxi service, Ashford."

I ground my teeth. "My car's a wreck and I haven't got a ride. It's important."

"Well, in that case… you'll owe me one."

Chapter 43

DEBBIE SCREECHED the patrol car to a halt on the road outside Linda McKenzie's house. There was no sign of Deepa.

"I can't see my partner."

"She must have left with the officers. Shall we have a look around?"

"Yes, let's do that." I noticed no officers had stayed in case McKenzie returned home. O'Toole had scattered them around the nearby suburbs looking for her. She might have come back or be hiding somewhere. "Have you got a gun, Debbie?"

"Of course." She pulled her Glock 17 from a holster as she got out of the car. "Have you? You'd better say 'no', Danny."

"No." By law, only the police were permitted guns, but the shotgun hung secretly in a deep inside pocket of my raincoat.

I got out of the car into the chill wind.

And then I saw it. Deepa's scooter, lying on its side in the gutter on the other side of the road.

A cold shiver knifed through me. A spike of adrenaline coursed through my veins. Heart pounding, I ran across the road. A car's horn blared. I'd forgotten to check if the road was clear.

Deepa's phone lay on the ground beside the scooter's front wheel. Now I knew why she hadn't answered it. The screen hadn't broken. I scooped it up and thrust it into a pocket. Nervous sweat beaded on my forehead.

Something had happened to Deepa. Heat rushed into my cheeks as the initial shock turned to anger.

Debbie called out. "Danny! What's going on?"

"Deepa's not here. Linda must have got her. Call for backup. We've got to find Deepa."

"There is no backup. Everyone's already out looking for the murderer."

I heard the words but didn't register what she was saying. I heaved the scooter upright. The key remained in the ignition. Good.

Where would that bitch have taken Deepa? Somewhere she knew no one would disturb her. Panic grabbed at my heart. Linda might already be there, wherever it was, doing whatever she wanted to Deepa. Hurting her. Maybe Deepa was already dead.

I had an idea of where to look. I swung my leg over the scooter and switched on the ignition. How hard could this thing be to ride? It looked easy when Deepa did it.

Debbie shouted something, but I didn't take in any of the words. I revved the engine. The scooter shot forward into the road and across the centre line. I squeezed the brake and the scooter's back wheel skidded on the wet, greasy surface. Debbie leaped to one side.

Somehow, I stayed on. I reduced the engine revs, found an approximate centre of gravity, and crossed back onto the proper side of the road. Then I accelerated. The cold wind breezed in my hair and on the anxious sweat on my forehead.

Would I make it in time?

Chapter 44

THE JOURNEY TO Fallswell and beyond seemed to take forever. I took every corner as fast as the Vespa would allow without losing traction. I only stopped at the occasional red light. The other red lights I whizzed through.

I skidded to a stop outside the property where Bronwyn Dodd, at that time Bronwyn Lewis, had lived with her former partner and her daughter, Linda McKenzie, seven years ago. It was an old wooden house, set back from the road amongst mature trees. A tall fence hid it from the road apart from the driveway entrance.

I parked the scooter on the footpath where it couldn't be seen from the house, and made my way into the grounds, keeping to the shadows of the trees. As I got closer to the building, I paused every so often to listen. There was only the rustle of wind in the trees and the sounds of birds overhead.

Could I be wrong? Was I wasting my time poking around an empty property, when McKenzie had taken Deepa elsewhere? My stomach heaved. If I'd made a mistake, put Deepa in danger and failed to save her, then whatever evil befell her would be my fault. How could I live with that?

I weaved between more trees, heading to the right of the property. The rear of the navy-blue station wagon came into view parked behind the house. I'd been unable to see it until I got close and moved around the side.

There was a garage or large shed back there too. It was far enough from the road, and from any neighbours, for anyone to hear what happened in there. A chill ran through my entire body. Was Deepa alive? Would I be in time?

I ran, stooped over, to the wall of the garage. I waited for a few moments to catch my breath and listen. Nothing. I edged around the side of the building to the front. It was an old-style garage with wooden double doors. They were barely ajar, letting in some light. An internal source of light was on, but from my angle I couldn't see anything except part of the garage wall.

They had to be in there.

I pulled the shotgun from my pocket and double-checked that it was loaded. Four shots, if I needed them. And I might, as I'd only had one firearms training lesson. During that, I'd only hit the stationary target twenty percent of the time. If I had to shoot at McKenzie, she might be moving and shooting back.

It always looked easy in the movies. Actors fired high-calibre weapons with no recoil and complete accuracy.

But this wasn't a movie. My hand shook.

I listened at the gap in the door. Deepa was speaking. I couldn't make out her words, but I relaxed. She was alive.

A different voice, a female's, crying. That had to be McKenzie. I cocked my head. What was going on?

Feet stamped as the voice cried out. "Why, why?"

The shotgun sat uncomfortably in my hands. I raised it, held it level and eased the door open with my foot.

It creaked as if no one had oiled the hinges for decades.

McKenzie spun. She spotted me as I moved inside. The garage was enormous, more like a small barn, but mostly empty. Dust motes swirled in the light penetrating the dirty side windows. Twine bound Deepa to a simple chair, the hard-seated kind that schools used to have to torture their student's bums. McKenzie stood beside Deepa, distraught. Her focus snapped back when she saw me. Eight to ten metres stretched between us.

"Don't move! Put your hands where I can see them."

McKenzie ignored me and darted behind the chair, crouching down, using Deepa as cover. Deepa jolted the chair sideways. It started to topple, but McKenzie righted it and held it firm.

"McKenzie, it's all over. Give yourself up."

She began crying again. "Why this? Why this?"

I lowered my gun. It was no use in this situation. I couldn't fire it in Deepa's direction, not with my poor aim and an unsteady hand.

McKenzie appeared to be having some kind of emotional fit. "Why am I here?" Her voice was soft, almost unvoiced, like a child's high-pitched whisper. It was chilling.

"What did you say?"

She didn't answer and sat on the floor.

Deepa trembled. "I thought she was going to kill me. Then I told her about her mother and everything we learned from her, and she just broke down crying."

"Why am I here?" McKenzie sat sobbing like a kid who'd just lost her best friend. Or her beloved dog.

I took another step closer. We could end this without bloodshed if I was careful. "Calm down, Linda. Let's talk about this."

"I'm Helen."

Chapter 45

"HELEN?" Who the hell was Helen?

It hit me. Different voice, different personality. Helen sounded like a child, a fragmented identity of a little girl with a terrible mother who'd just lost her only friend, her dog Friendly. Linda was the woman, the antique clock repairer, Bronwyn's daughter, who could only move forward by forcing the emotional horror of her youth into the child sub-personality that she could usually ignore. Except in times of stress. Like when she came across Chris Dodd again

Deepa stared at me with eyes wide, pleading for me to get her away from her captor.

Helen wailed, distressed, almost toppling over. "Keep away from me. Oh, my head hurts."

"I can help you." I took another step towards her.

"No closer! I have a gun." McKenzie's voice changed, and was no longer that of the timid child, but deeper, more confident, that of a woman. Linda's voice. Her words echoed off the walls.

The gun must have been behind the chair, and she'd picked it up. I could see the barrel pointing safely downwards.

"It's Linda, isn't it? You have to give yourself up. There's no way out of this. The police are on their way." I lied. Of course, they weren't on their way. I hadn't told anyone where I was going when I rushed here.

Linda spoke again. "Stay where you are. I don't want anyone to get hurt. This isn't my fault, you understand? I didn't do this."

"You bloody did." Deepa kicked back and clipped her shins, but with no force. McKenzie didn't react.

I could still end this without violence. Save the situation. Save *Deepa*.

"Linda, where's Helen?" I talked calmly, assessing McKenzie's response.

"Helen can't handle things like this. That's why I'm here, to protect her. She's always needed protection." Linda spoke in a level, rational tone.

"Protection from what, Linda?"

"The drunken beatings from her mother's partner. The emotional abuse, and worse, from the postman when her mother's partner wasn't around—or when he was too drunk to wake up. The unrelenting cold negativity and hatred from her mother. The death of Friendly, her dog and only friend in the world. Her mother leaving her without saying goodbye and never contacting her again. The taunts from the postman that she'd never come back. The postman coming in the house, coming to see Helen."

Deepa gasped. I swallowed, my chest tight, my mind reeling as I tried to comprehend this.

Linda remembered the horrors of her childhood—cognitively. She buried the emotions in the Helen child sub-personality she created as a whipping-girl identity, a persona to suffer in her place, because she couldn't cope with them herself. Helen was the fragmented part of Linda who never grew up and still feels the pain.

My heart wrenched at the thought. But I had to put that aside. I had to save Deepa.

I took a step closer to be within range of charging McKenzie if I had to. "The postman? You mean Chris Dodd?"

"Yes, that's him."

"So, that's why Helen was crying?"

"Yes."

"What the hell? Will someone get me out of here?" Deepa strained at her bonds.

"Release her, Linda."

"Not yet. I have to think of a way out of this situation first. It isn't my fault, you understand?"

I still held my shotgun, lowered. "Can I speak to Helen, please, Linda?"

"That's not possible."

"What's not possible?" I had to keep cool, though this was exasperating. I needed to get Deepa away from this woman.

"You can't speak to Helen. This is too much stress for her. I protect Helen. Fix things up for her. Work. Pay the bills. Be nice to people."

"You call this being nice? If you want to be nice, you can untie me, you bitch." Deepa struggled in vain.

"Deepa, take some deep breaths. I need you to calm yourself down. You're reacting like this because of the shock."

"Of course I am!"

My mind whirled as what Linda had said sunk in. She was protecting the child Helen from harm, but in reality, Helen protected Linda by bearing all the hurt and pain of her abusive childhood. Oh, the irony. How twisted and how sad. How utterly, terribly heart-wrenching.

My head swam in this psychological murkiness for a few moments until I refocused. Deepa was captive, in danger. I had to get to her.

I edged forward until I was about five metres away.

Linda held up a hand. "Don't come any closer. I don't want anyone to get hurt. I only want to get out of here."

Deepa swung her head round. "Bloody hell. Why did you bring me here, then?"

"It wasn't me. I *told* you. It was Gerry."

Now we were getting somewhere, but Gerry was someone I didn't want to talk to. Linda at least seemed rational. I no longer wanted to talk with Helen. I could fix this situation with Linda.

Deepa looked at me, aghast. "You were right about the multiple personalities, Danny. I didn't fully believe you until now. I thought it was one of your over-thought psychological profiling ideas."

"Thanks a lot, Deepa." The sarcasm dripped from my voice like treacle.

"You think you understand me?" McKenzie snarled. "You don't understand."

"Tell us, then, Linda. Help us to understand."

Deepa glared at me as if to remind me she was tied to a chair and she wanted me to do something about it. But I was playing for time. The longer I could spin out the conversation with Linda, the greater the chance that I could talk her into giving herself up without anyone getting hurt.

"Helen is a sensitive kid. She was… mistreated. Unloved. Made to feel worth less than shit. I came along to protect her from all that when everything got too hard, when the worst things were said and done to her. When her mother left—as horrible as she was, she was better than her partner. When Helen's dog, Friendly, was put down, Helen had nothing left to live for. I looked after her, so she wouldn't harm herself."

"Helen's about eight? Ten?"

"Eight."

So, the Helen personality is much younger than Linda was when her dog was put down, the postman abused her, her mother left and her mother's partner committed suicide. And Linda's tortured mind had created that little girl sub-personality and stuffed all into it all the horrors and emotions she couldn't deal with herself, for personal survival.

It was a lot to take in. "And do you and Helen get on well together? Or not?"

Deepa stared at me as if I were speaking a foreign language.

"It's complicated. I don't talk to Helen. I look after her. She doesn't even know about me."

"You're the dominant identity."

"I have to be. Helen's a child. She couldn't survive without me."

"You mean, you couldn't have survived without her. Helen is a split-up part of you that has to live with the terrible memories of your past, so you—Linda—could grow up and survive." But Linda herself wasn't to blame for this. Her subconscious mind had worked to save her by creating the sub-personas containing all the fear and hate that Linda herself couldn't face.

"What?" Linda stared at me with a blank expression, biting her lip.

"Do you remember how you feel about your childhood, Linda? Your adolescence?"

"Um…"

I changed tack. "Sometimes Helen… takes over?"

Linda nodded. She hadn't yet relaxed her grip on the shotgun. "Yes. And then I have blackouts."

"Blackouts? You mean periods of missing time?"

"Yes. When one of the others takes over. I don't remember those times."

"That must be hard, Linda."

"Yes. It is." Her head drooped forward as if a wave of sadness had come over her.

"We can get you help. It doesn't have to be like this."

"No one can help me." A plaintive tone now. Was it Helen? Her voice had changed; it was no longer the confident tone of Linda, but the higher-pitched squeak of a child who would never grow up, and never leave her pain behind.

I called out gently. "Helen?"

"Why am I here? What's going on? Where am I?" She snapped at me as if it was my fault.

"I'll answer all that for you, Helen. Just put the gun on the floor and move away."

"No. You got a gun, so I'll keep my gun too. You can't make me put it down."

"Okay, Helen, I'll put my gun down. Look, I'm putting it on the floor." I did so, then kicked it away from me to the side, making sure it wasn't going in her direction.

"I'm not putting my gun down. So there. You're bad people. You brought me here, didn't you?"

This was too much for Deepa. "What the hell? You kidnapped me! You stuffed me in your car."

"I can't even drive, miss."

I tried to appeal to her common sense. "Helen, think about it. If we brought you here, why is my friend tied up?"

She pointed the gun at me, and I tensed. I could see it clearly now: a seventeen-shot Mossberg pump-action shotgun, gleaming black, in the hands of a killer with the mind of a child. If only Linda would come back.

"You must've brought me and her to this place. You're the bad one."

"That's not true." I shook my head.

"He's my friend and partner." Deepa sounded kindlier now. Either she was following my lead, or she'd realized the mental suffering our perp was under.

McKenzie's gaze darted from Deepa to me and back again. Her grip on the shotgun wavered. Her bottom lip quivered. She shuddered, fingers trembling around the trigger.

The gun went off with a roar and a cloud of smoke. Deepa screamed. I spun. A hole in the wall showed where the slug had passed through, a little to the left of me.

I turned back to face McKenzie. She stood straighter, taller, and meaner, her chin jutting forward with an arrogant scowl. She sauntered around to Deepa's left-hand side, pumping the shotgun as she did so, ejecting the empty cartridge and loading a new one from the magazine. The click-clack sound was like thunder in the silence after the shot. The clink of the empty cartridge hitting the concrete floor set my teeth on edge.

McKenzie levelled the shotgun at the side of Deepa's head.

Deepa stared at me, wide-eyed, imploring me to do something. But I was too far away to dash forward. Nor could I reach my gun. McKenzie could fire the shotgun in a fraction of a second.

McKenzie nodded vigorously as if she'd made up her mind about something, then spoke. "You fucking bitch. You should never have written that shit about me. I'm going to blow your fucking head off."

Her guttural voice was deeper and gravelly. This wasn't Helen or Linda.

It was Gerry. The male identity.

The killer.

Chapter 46

I CRIED OUT in desperation. "Wait! Don't shoot her. Listen to me."

Gerry swivelled towards me, eyes narrowed. "Why should I?"

I swallowed, then exhaled. I'd been holding my breath.

Gerry swung the weapon in my direction, holding it with both hands, steadying it, ready to fire. I stared down its barrel. At least it wasn't pointing at Deepa now. But what next? How were we going to get out of this situation? How could I stop McKenzie—Gerry—from going on a killing spree, starting with us?

"Deepa can write your story. Your words, your past, what's happened to you. Whatever you want to say in the *Richter Mail* for all of Quake City to read."

Gerry cocked his head. "Anything I want to say, she'll write for the newspaper?"

"Yes. So, you can't kill her because then you won't have anyone to write your story for you. Only Deepa can do that." I was hoping he'd believe this nonsense.

"Yeah, I guess you're right. But I don't need you."

Gerry braced himself for the sharp recoil. I dived to my right and rolled as a blast tore another hole in the back wall behind where I'd been. In a moment, I regained my feet, my four-shot Remington shotgun back in my hands. I pointed it at Gerry before he could recover his balance.

"Don't move. Drop your weapon, Gerry."

He grinned. "No fucking way. You won't shoot." He swung the shotgun in a slow-motion arc until it was pointing straight at me.

He was right. I couldn't shoot. I might hit Deepa.

Gerry laughed a deep, belly-graunch kind of laugh that didn't sound human, let alone from the vocal cords of a woman.

I tensed.

Deepa took her chance. Now that Gerry wasn't holding her chair, she pushed off with both feet, making the chair hop in his direction. It barged into him, knocking him off balance. A chair leg drove onto his right foot.

He screamed. "You've broken my toe!"

Gerry swiped at Deepa with the butt of the shotgun. She ducked, and the chair tipped over. His blow sailed over where her head had been moments before. I barrelled into him, sending us both flying. My gun skittered across the floor in one direction, while my chin led my skid in another.

Bad move.

Gerry got to his feet unsteadily, his eyes blazing. Somehow, he'd kept hold of the shotgun. He raised it, grimacing in pain.

Gerry grabbed the side of his head, paused, then snivelled. Not the sound of physical pain, but of emotional distress, a child's anguish.

"Tell my story." She turned and hobbled out of the garage, still carrying the weapon. Linda or Helen. Her teeth clenched against the pain of her broken toe muffled her voice, and I wasn't sure exactly who it was.

Deepa kicked the floor and called out, her voice strangled. "Help me. I can't breathe."

I jumped to my feet and rushed over to Deepa. She was on the floor, the chair on top of her, pressing into the back of her neck. I pulled the chair upright, releasing the pressure.

There wasn't anything suitable to cut the twine with, so I struggled with the knots. A Swiss Army knife leapt to the top of my wish list.

Thirty seconds later, I'd loosened the twine enough so Deepa could fling it off. I raced to the double doors, but too late. I swung them open to see the station wagon accelerating down the driveway, tyres spitting gravel.

I spun, groaning. "She's got away."

Deepa scooped up her laptop bag, which had been lying on the floor next to the wall. She grabbed my shotgun and shoved it inside. The barrel poked out of the top. "How'd you get here? You got a car?"

"I rode your scooter."

She joined me at the doors. "Where is it?"

"Out on the roadside."

"Hurry, then." She ran towards the road, laptop bag thumping at her side. I followed, but I couldn't keep up. Deepa was much fitter than me.

Deepa reached the scooter twenty seconds before me and swung her leg over. "Where's the key?"

"I've got it." I was breathless. When I got nearer, I pulled the key from my pocket and threw it to her. She grabbed it and jabbed it into the ignition while I came to a stop next to her. I remembered her phone and handed it over to her. She stuffed it into her jacket pocket.

We were almost ready to scoot off—but we didn't know where to go.

"Where's do you think she's gone?" The rising tone of desperation rang from Deepa's voice.

"Where have *they* gone, you mean?" I panted, trying to get my breath back. "It depends on which personality is dominant at the moment."

"She won't go home, right? She knows we're on to her."

"Agreed. We need to figure out likely places, and contact Inspector O'Toole. He's got everyone out looking for McKenzie in the area around her house."

"So, in the wrong place."

"Yes. Tell me, what were you saying to McKenzie before I arrived? I heard her crying."

Deepa's hand went to her mouth, a sign of realization. "She seemed disorientated. I'd been trying to calm her down, and it was working. You know, it was Gerry who grabbed me, stuffed me in the car trunk and brought me here. He—he was going to kill me, Danny."

I took a deep breath. "I know. When you talked about McKenzie's mother, he must have switched to Helen."

"Yep, she rambled on about her dog, and that postman, Chris Dodd, who had the dog put down. She talked about abuse from Dodd and neglect from her mother and mother's partner. I promised to write her story and make sure the world knew what a dirt ball Chris Dodd was. She deserved this for what she'd suffered."

"Good idea."

"I told her that her mother went to live with Dodd and married him. She didn't know that. Bronwyn had kept her relationship with Dodd a secret, then abandoned her partner and Helen and never saw either of them again. When I told her, she went to pieces. That's when she started crying, and you arrived shortly afterwards."

"Right. I expect she's gone to Dodd's house to confront her mother."

"Oh, shit. What do you think she's going to do?"

"The question is: who's she going to *be* when she's there?"

I called O'Toole and let him know what we'd discovered. The inspector listened, then said he and Amy would be on their way with some armed officers. I thanked him and disconnected.

"He said we should keep out of the way. Let's hurry, so we can get there before them."

"Is that a good idea?"

I gave Deepa my deadpan face. "You wanted me to get you a story. This is it. We need to be there to be part of it. Besides, they might need our help. The police will be too slow. We're nearby. We can stop another murder happening."

"She's a bitch."

"I know. But we can't simply sit here doing nothing."

"Get on, then." Deepa switched on the ignition and revved the engine while I swung my leg over and mounted the scooter behind her. I'd barely settled into place when the Vespa shot forward. With one foot sliding on the road, Deepa swivelled the scooter around one hundred and eighty degrees on a tight turn. Then she straightened up and accelerated.

Chapter 47

PRECIOUS MINUTES PASSED while Deepa navigated the traffic as fast as she dared—damned fast, actually. I clung tight whenever she made sharp turns. The wheels left the road when we hit speed bumps at three times the advised limit. We took a shortcut across a footbridge over the river, and minutes later arrived at Dodd's house.

I'd been there a lot lately.

McKenzie's station wagon was on the front lawn, mostly hidden by the tall front fence. Deepa rode in and skidded the scooter to a stop on the grass. I lost my balance, tumbled off and rolled to my feet. Deepa kicked the foot stand on the Vespa while I ran to the house.

The front door was open. I slowed, unsure whether to dash in or tread quietly.

Deepa ran up onto the wooden porch beside me. "See anything?" Her laptop bag banged against the house. We no longer had the quiet option.

"Nothing. No sign of them in the living room or the hall. I was about to go in."

Shouting erupted from the back yard.

Deepa and I glanced at each other.

"Stay here." I knew she wouldn't.

I took off at a run around the house. I was half way when I realised that I couldn't hear her footsteps behind me.

I reached the corner of the house leading to the back yard. To my left was an old single garage, a woodshed and some garden furniture. Bronwyn Dodd sat on a chair, shock on her face at the sight of her daughter, Linda

McKenzie—or one of her alter identities—who stood a few paces away with the Mossberg levelled at Bronwyn.

The tension was so intense it felt as if the earth itself could crack open.

McKenzie spoke, spittle flying from her mouth. "Why did you do it, Mummy? Why did you go away to be with that man who killed Friendly? Why did you leave me behind?"

It was Helen. The child identity. I gulped. She couldn't be reasoned with.

Bronwyn stood and raised her chin defiantly. "I was sick of living in that shit hole with that waste of space of a partner and you always under my feet. You were such a snively little kid, always hanging onto my skirt. Unable to do anything for yourself. It was time you learnt to stand on your own two feet. Chris was a stupid bastard, but he had a nice house and bought me things…"

McKenzie's lip quivered. Her breathing increased, and she closed her eyes for a long moment. Then she stood straighter and grinned widely. "It was me. I killed the fucker. I killed your husband. He deserved it for what he did to me."

Now this was Gerry. I had to put a stop to this before Gerry killed Bronwyn too. I stepped out from behind the edge of the house into full view, digging in my pocket for my Glock 17.

It wasn't there. *Damnation.*

My stomach lurched. I'd brought the Remington, but I didn't have it now. It was in Deepa's bag.

But there was no going back now. I raised both my hands. "Gerry. Stop. Put the gun down. You don't want to do this. Don't make things worse for yourself." Though McKenzie was in enough trouble as it was, Gerry might not care, or might think that killing another person wouldn't make a lot of difference to his current body count. Hopefully, though, it wouldn't be me.

"You again." He bared his teeth and kept the gun pointed toward Bronwyn.

Bronwyn took a step or two back, hand over heart, as if in shock. "You killed Chris?"

Gerry's focus snapped back to Bronwyn. "He squealed for his life first. He begged. I enjoyed killing that turd. He fucking deserved it."

Bronwyn didn't respond. She stood there unblinkingly.

"I wanted you to know that before I kill you." The corners of Gerry's mouth turned down.

I sensed something was poised to happen in moments. I had to stop it. "Wait! Let's talk about this." Bronwyn wasn't mother of the year, but she didn't deserve to die.

"Enough talking."

I kept my gaze on Gerry. His grip on the shotgun hadn't loosened, but his finger wasn't moving off the trigger guard onto the trigger itself. And the safety switch on the top of the gun was on.

Gerry wasn't going to shoot his mother after all.

Bronwyn turned and marched the few steps to the side door of the garage, opened it and reached inside for something. She turned swiftly, raising a shotgun of her own.

They stood there, fifteen paces apart, guns pointed at each other, like two gunslingers in an old Western movie, with deadly intent.

This couldn't go on. Where were the police? Were they coming here on bicycles or something?

"Stop! Both of you, put your guns down."

They ignored me. Something was happening to Gerry. He slouched forward and dropped to his knees, lowering the gun to the grass and putting his hands to his head. "Mummy, why?"

Helen, again. She scrunched up her face as if she was about to burst into tears. With the immense stress of the situation, all the identities were fighting each other for control, and none of them could hold onto it for long.

I breathed easier. Gerry had gone, at least for now.

"This is for my husband." Bronwyn's expression hardened.

The gun roared. The slug hit McKenzie in the chest, throwing her backwards, arms splayed. Blood spread across her blouse. Her glazed eyes stared at the sky as a trickle of blood ran from her mouth into the grass.

"What have you done?" I stared in astonishment. I hadn't foreseen this.

Bronwyn pivoted the gun towards me. "No witnesses." She pumped the action on her shotgun.

Chapter 48

I CLOSED MY EYES. A blast rang out. It sounded as if it came from my right. After a moment, I worked out I wasn't dead, or even injured, and opened my eyes.

Bronwyn lay on the grass, her weapon at her side, shot through the upper chest. Like McKenzie, her eyes were already lifeless.

Deepa stood by the other corner of the house, holding the Remington. Wisps of smoke confirmed that she'd fired the fatal slug. The shot that had saved my life.

I rushed to her, took the gun from her, and pulled her into my arms. She trembled, then sobbed against my shoulder.

I hugged her, almost crying myself. "Thank you. Without you, I'd be dead."

She pulled back and wiped her eyes. "But, Danny, I killed someone. What am I going to do?"

Sirens sounded in the distance, approaching rapidly. *Now* the police were arriving, when it was all over.

"Don't worry, Deepa, we can take care of this."

"I'll plead self-defence. She was going to shoot you."

I shook my head. "That's not necessary. We'll say they shot each other. That's what it looks like, doesn't it?"

"Does it?"

"Yes. Her gun's already been fired. Give me the Remington."

Deepa handed it over. Her face was pale, he was shaking, and her voice was a despairing whisper. "Hurry."

I stuffed the shotgun into the deep inner pocket of my raincoat where it wouldn't be seen, and put my arm around Deepa's shoulders, consoling her.

The sirens stopped. Seconds later, the first armed officers ran around the corner of the house, followed by O'Toole and Amy Ling.

"What in hell's name happened here?" The inspector came to a halt at the corner of the house, taking in the whole bloody scene.

The armed officers lowered their weapons and called for medics. It was far too late for medics, though.

I faced O'Toole and kept my voice level. "We got here too late. It looks like they shot each other."

Deepa stayed silent, but turned her face into my shoulder.

A medic rushed to her with a warm blanket. "Let's get you to the ambulance."

Deepa clung to my raincoat, not letting go. "I'm not going anywhere. I'm all right. Just a little shaken."

The medic returned to her colleague, who was fetching covers for the two bodies. Amy was on her phone, asking for the coroner.

O'Toole sauntered over. "Superb work, Ashford. You tracked down a serial killer. The best thing is we're saved the cost and trouble of a trial. But what happened with Bronwyn Dodd?"

"She's Linda's mother. They haven't seen each other since she abandoned McKenzie seven years ago."

"What a mess." O'Toole sighed. "Well, I suppose I'd better go tell the superintendent about this, wrap up the paperwork for this case, and move on to the next one."

"Wait, Inspector. There's more."

"More? You mean there are more serial killers after all?"

"No, not that. There's something that's been bothering me about this case, about our first victim, Ricky Cohen."

"The postman sharing the route with Chris Dodd. What about him?"

Amy finished with her call to the coroner and came over to join us. Deepa turned to participate—or gather material for another article.

I explained. "It was too much of a coincidence that they shared the same postal route and were killed a day apart. Then Deepa found out that

McKenzie had a motive for killing Chris Dodd—Dodd had her childhood dog, her only friend, put down."

"All right. What about Cohen, then? He was killed first."

Amy, never one to talk much, nodded.

I continued. "Once we knew that, it seemed like Dodd was McKenzie's real target. So, I asked myself, why kill Ricky Cohen? Was it a case of mistaken identity?"

"Seems reasonable."

Deepa joined the conversation. "Or McKenzie could have killed Cohen as a warm-up to the main event. Convince herself that she could go through with it."

"Different M.O.s, though." O'Toole scratched his head. "And what about the other murders? I'm thinking about a copycat serial killer here."

"No, Inspector." I shook my head vehemently. "McKenzie was responsible for all of them. She had a multiple personality disorder. Her violent sub-persona Gerry—"

"The killer's name from the appeals call. So, that wasn't Linda McKenzie, then?"

"No. I believe Gerry's identity surfaced to carry out the murders. By the time he'd killed Cohen and Dodd, he was hooked on the bloodlust, and his crimes became more audacious and deranged. And he had an absolute hatred of postmen in general. In fact, he despised anyone delivering any kind of message or talking about him. But Cohen was a different matter altogether."

"Okay… I'm following you with this, Ashford, but in what way was Cohen different? He was a postman too. You said it was mistaken identity or a warm-up murder, maybe one to throw us off the scent of the actual target. It was the same postal route and all that."

"I think they were *both* targets, Inspector. What I think happened is that McKenzie saw Dodd delivering the mail. The shock and distress at seeing her abuser again brought forth the Gerry identity, who decided to kill him."

"They were both targets?" The inspector's eyebrows rose and his eyes widened.

"There's more to it, and for that we need to talk to Bernice Cohen."

"All right. I hope your instincts are on track."

Deepa eyed me, her head at an incline.

"Let's go. You'll want this for your exclusive story."

"I wouldn't miss it. Though I think I've already got enough for a double feature."

"Meet you there." O'Toole and Amy walked to one of the police cars while we returned to Deepa's scooter, leaving the SOCO investigators going over the scene in the back yard.

Chapter 49

I TOLD DEEPA TO make a brief detour. We stopped on a quiet street in Riverside. I swung my leg over the scooter, strode over to the shrubbery at the riverbank, stepped through, and dropped the Remington into the river. It sank, nestling itself in the muddy bottom at the edge of the bank.

We arrived at the Cohen's house and stopped outside the house next door. O'Toole and Amy were already there. We met them at the gate and advanced up the pathway to the front door in pairs.

The living room curtain twitched.

I rapped on the door.

After a moment, Louise Slater, Bernice's sister, answered. "Have you caught the killer?"

"We have, yes." Inspector O'Toole glanced at me, and I nodded to him to continue. "May we come inside? We have some more questions for you."

Amy got out her police notebook.

We went in, and Louise showed us into the living room, where we took seats on the sofa and chairs. Bernice sat at the dining table, leafing through a cruise line brochure. I glanced at the time.

"Bernice, the inspector said they have caught the killer."

Bernice sat up straight. "Wonderful."

"Unfortunately, we didn't capture her alive." O'Toole almost looked apologetic.

I frowned. I hadn't wanted them to know that.

"Her?" Bernice's eyebrows rose. "At least that's justice for my poor dead husband." Then her expression fell, and a tear slid down her cheek. She wiped it away.

I glanced at the certificates on the wall commemorating Bernice Cohen's achievements: naturopathy, acupuncture, amateur dramatics. "Did you know Linda McKenzie?"

Both women shook their heads.

"Are you planning a trip somewhere?" I pointed at the cruise brochures.

"Those? Oh, you know, Louise suggested a trip away together might help me with my grief."

O'Toole gave me a measured glance and leaned over to whisper in my ear. "What's going on, Ashford? What are you up to?"

"You'll know in a minute, Inspector. Literally."

"I'd better."

I looked around. Deepa was scribbling notes. Amy wasn't. She stared at me as if she wondered what we were all doing here.

Louise spoke up. "It's been a tough day. A tough few days. If you don't have any further questions...?" She stood, indicating she wanted to terminate the interview.

The cuckoo clock sounded the half-hour.

Amy swivelled her head. "I know that sound. It was on one of the calls following the public appeal."

"Yes, it was, and I'll tell you why that's important." Everyone's attention turned to me. "It was in a call in which a woman with a disguised voice stated that Linda McKenzie was the killer." I looked from Louise to Bernice. "Which one of you two made the call?"

Louise spluttered. "How ridiculous. Why would we do that? We—"

Bernice talked over her. "We don't even know that person. And there must be a lot of cuckoo clocks in Quake City."

I stood and went over to the wall by the clock. "This is a Black Forest cuckoo clock, according to this label. They have a unique sound, and I'm certain we will be able to match the sound of this clock perfectly to that on the recorded appeals call."

Louise, still standing, clamped her mouth shut, frowning. Bernice slumped back in her chair.

"What I'm thinking is this: you met Linda McKenzie somewhere. Maybe she even came to the house and fixed your clock or valued it. Maybe you told her that Ricky was a postman."

In my peripheral vision I saw Deepa tilting her head from side to side in that idiosyncratic manner of hers. She and I knew that Linda—and her sub-personas—had issues with postmen.

"Somehow you got into a discussion about your life or future plans, how unhappy you were in your marriage, Bernice."

"Why on earth would I discuss something like that with a stranger?"

I indicated the fading purplish bruise on her face. "Maybe she noticed that bruise. You didn't do that walking into a door, did you? Ricky did that to you, didn't he?"

Bernice was silent. Louise inclined her head. They both gave me their full attention.

"Then McKenzie offered to kill him for you. Am I right?" Though it would have been Gerry, of course. Maybe this was the trigger that brought Gerry's identity to the surface, recognising abuse from a postman, a reminder of the hurt from years ago.

Bernice protested, but I held up my hand to stop her. "You entered into an arrangement to pay McKenzie to kill your husband, and you'd collect the generous insurance pay-out on Ricky's life and start a new future, richer and without the ball and chain of a husband you no longer loved."

"That's outrageous."

"Then you named her on the appeals line, saying she's dangerous and should be shot on sight. Of course, then she wouldn't be able to tell the police you hired her as a hitman. I mean, a hitwoman. Isn't that right?"

"Preposterous." Bernice's voice was a murmur. "Maybe I didn't love Ricky anymore, but I'd never do that to him. We still liked each other."

O'Toole whispered in my ear. "This is dammed far-fetched. Look, we've got the killer, why don't we call it a day? We might never prove anything about this, even if you're right."

"Inspector, I'm sure one or both of them is involved." I had one hand covering the side of my mouth to prevent the sisters overhearing.

Amy walked into the hall, dialling on her phone. I waited. Deepa whispered in my other ear. I didn't catch what she said because Louise had piped up, complaining vociferously about my accusations.

Louise stopped complaining and shifted uncomfortably on her feet. "Anyone want a hot drink?"

"No, thanks." I didn't want to give Louise the chance to leave the room and make a run for it. Deepa gave the same reply. O'Toole appeared to be about to ask for a cup of tea, but changed his mind following my meaningful glance.

Amy returned. "I've been on the phone to headquarters. Debbie looked up some things for me. There was a fifteen-thousand-dollar deposit in cash into McKenzie's bank account ten days ago."

Deepa tilted her head. "Wouldn't the bank have brought that to the attention of the police?"

"They probably did, and nothing happened in whichever department received that information." These things frequently slipped past the inattentive and lazy Quake City police.

Amy glared at me as if she could read my thoughts. "The same amount of cash had been taken out of Louise Slater's account at a different bank twenty minutes earlier."

Bernice took a sharp intake of breath and turned to her sister. "You—you didn't, you can't have… say it isn't true."

It was Louise? I'd thought it was Bernice, or the two of them together. But had Louise acted alone? Had she orchestrated it all?

"What do you have to say to this?" O'Toole advanced towards Louise.

"It–it wasn't just me. It was her idea." Louse pointed at Bernice. "We were going to collect the insurance and pension money and live it up together."

Bernice sat upright and folded her arms. "What utter tripe."

Louise bolted, dashing past me before I had a chance to react. She shoved Amy out of the way. Amy bounced off the door frame into the hall, and Louise raced past.

Then Deepa was after her. I'd barely made it into the hall when I saw, through the open front door, Deepa bringing Louise to the ground with a tackle that would have turned the heads of some appreciative All Blacks.

I followed out to help hold down Louise's thrashing arms.

Amy followed, with O'Toole trundling after. "Louise Slater, I'm arresting you for conspiracy to murder Chris Dodd…"

Chapter 50

Day 7, late evening

TO CELEBRATE, Deepa and I went for dinner at the Drop Inn pub in Brittleton. Afterwards, at Deepa's suggestion, we strolled along the harbour front to the squawk of seagulls that hung around, probably hoping we would drop some chips for them. They were out of luck.

Deepa wore her purple puffer jacket. I wore a new fedora and my habitual raincoat, but it barely kept out the cold. This seemed such a terrible idea, freezing our butts off like this when we could have stayed in the pub or gone for a coffee somewhere, but I sensed that Deepa wanted to clear her head, and the cold, salty air helped. She'd killed a person, and I'd covered it up. Maybe she was having a harder time accepting that and moving on than I was.

We walked in silence for a few minutes before Deepa spoke.

"Danny?"

"Yes?"

"Do Black Forest cuckoo clocks really have a unique sound?"

I laughed. "I have no idea."

"So, you only said that to get a reaction? To suggest that the sound of the clock on the recording would match only their clock?"

"Yes. I'd never even heard of Black Forest cuckoo clocks until I checked the label on the side of their clock."

Deepa laughed and grabbed my arm. "That's so funny—and it worked."

"Not as funny as you tackling Louise when she tried to make a run for it.

She didn't even get as far as the gate."

"Do you think Bernice was involved too, like Louise claimed?"

"I'm pretty sure she was. Don't worry, she'll crack under police questioning and confess."

Deepa smiled. "We make excellent partners, you and I. We've been through such a lot together on this case."

"Yeah. We do make an exceptional team, don't we? You know, I didn't think we would, at the beginning."

"You didn't?"

"No, but your research and contacts, and just the way you… you're *there* all the time to talk to… it really helped."

"And I've written some of my best articles for the *Richter Mail* using your psychological profiling insights."

"Speaking of that—shouldn't you be writing an article now?"

"No. Don told me to take a day or two off. He'll run the regular articles tomorrow with the bare facts, and he's giving me a double-page feature spread for the full story of McKenzie's multiple personalities, how you solved the case—"

"How *we* solved the case, Deepa."

"We, then. I'll write about being kidnapped, then rescued by you, then how we caught up to her at the Dodds' house—though I'll repeat the story we told the police, of course."

"Good. That avoided… complications."

"Thank you."

"No problem." We walked further, still arm in arm, enjoying a companionable silence. Above us, stars gleamed. Water lapped at the harbour's edge. There was no one else around. Only the seagulls hadn't settled down for the night.

It was peaceful. I was having a marvellous time, walking arm in arm with this amazing woman who would stop at nothing to nail a significant story. And Deepa was damn good at investigating crime, too. Better than I'd expected. Would we do more cases together? Was this the start of a new business relationship?

Or maybe more? What about all those nights she stayed over at my apartment? Sure, it was because she didn't want the killer to track her down at her own place, but she stayed nevertheless. Did it mean things might change between us? Did I dare to think about that? And what would Torquemada think?

But whatever happened, Deepa had killed someone—albeit in self-defence—and we'd covered it up. That secret bound us together whether we liked it or not.

After a minute, I thought of something. "Deepa, did you have your phone on voice record when we were at the Dodd's house?"

"No."

"That's a relief."

"I recorded everything on the phone's video up until McKenzie got shot. Then I grabbed your shotgun from my bag."

I grimaced. "That's not good. The video's evidence."

"Oh. Should I have handed it in to the police?"

"Definitely not. It'll confirm that McKenzie didn't shoot her mother, that the shot came after she was dead. I don't want to take the chance of that video getting into the wrong hands. I mean, into police hands. Then we'll be in trouble for concealing evidence."

"What do you suggest?"

I stopped walking and disentangled myself from Deepa. "Hand me your phone."

She hesitated only a moment, reached into her jacket pocket for it, then passed it over.

It was a nice phone. The latest Samsung model. Expensive.

But incriminating.

With one fluid motion, I flung it as far as I could into the harbour. In the darkness, I couldn't see it, but I heard it splash some distance away.

"What the hell did you do that for? Do you know how much that phone cost?"

I shook my head. "It doesn't matter how much it cost. I don't want that video around. What if the police ask to see your phone? We'd have a lot to explain. But now it's gone, and the potential problem is gone with it."

"You idiot, Danny. The video's already been automatically uploaded to the cloud."

The what? "The cloud? Is that some reporter jargon?"

"No. My phone uploads all its photos and videos to storage on the internet. I have to delete the video from there if I want to remove it permanently. And even then, I don't know if it actually gets erased. You threw my phone into the sea for nothing." She stamped a foot.

I looked out into the harbour. Suddenly, I felt foolish.

"Sorry, Deepa, I didn't realize—"

"Then why didn't you ask first before destroying my phone?"

"Well, I…" I didn't know.

"Thanks a lot." She stormed off, laptop bag swinging against her hip.

I watched her go. Maybe she'd calm down a bit. It's just a phone. A phone that was worth a lot more than my old car, maybe, but a phone nevertheless.

She didn't turn around. After a minute or two, I followed. What an idiot I was. We'd been having a lovely time: dinner, a feeling of accomplishment and togetherness, a walk along the harbour—a *romantic* walk at that. And then I'd ruined it all by throwing her phone into the sea.

The familiar sound of a Vespa roaring into life came from up ahead. Deepa's scooter. The engine revved and then faded into the distance.

I was alone. The shadows closed in around me. The chilly air bit at my ears as I trudged along the waterfront towards the bus stop.

THE END

Reviews and more reading

If you liked this story, please consider leaving a review on Amazon to help other prospective readers decide if it's for them. Even a sentence or two will do.

Also, please consider following me on the sites below for details of my new releases:

Amazon

Bookbub

The series continues…

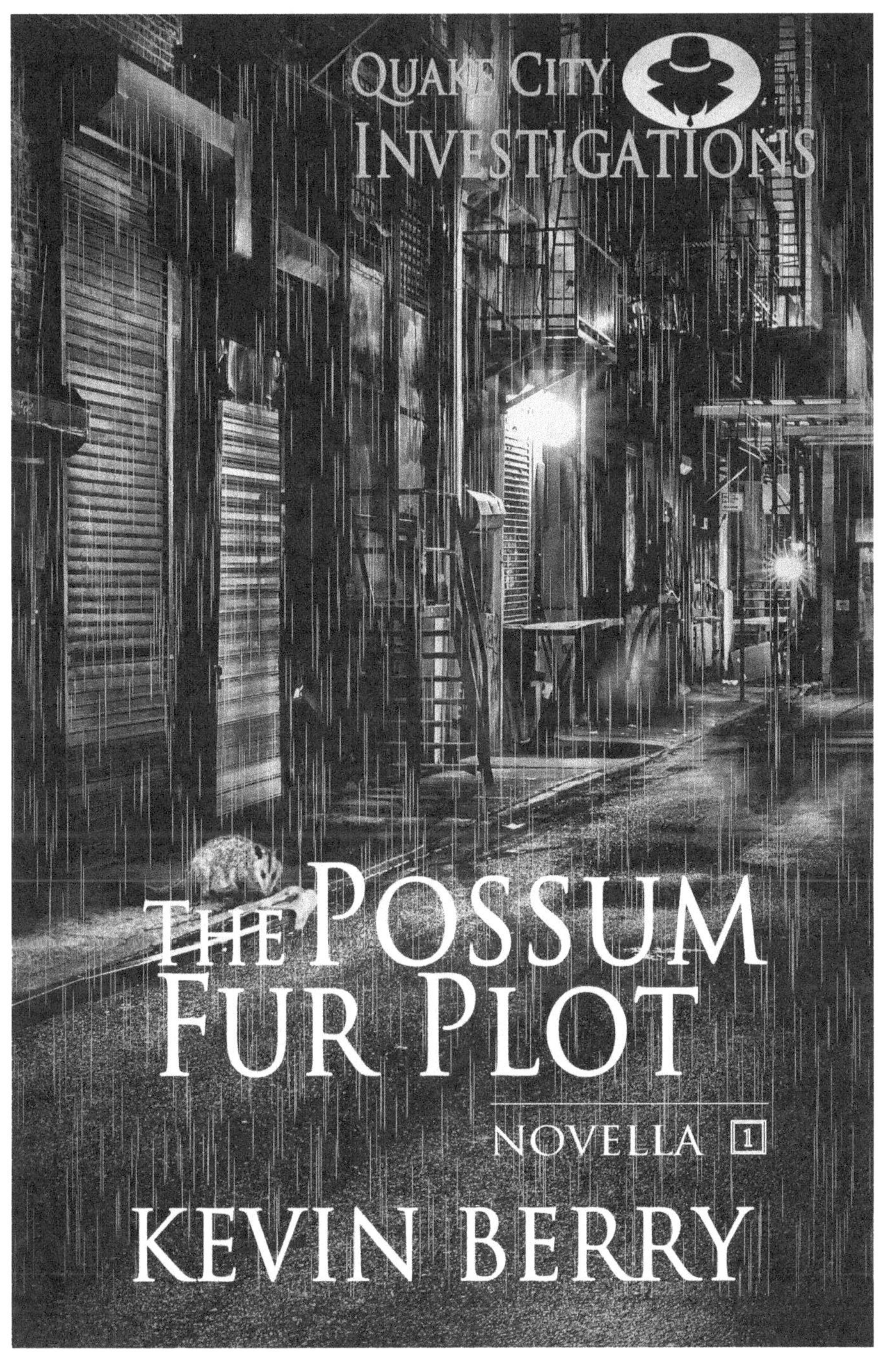

QUAKE CITY
INVESTIGATIONS
THE POSSUM
FUR PLOT
NOVELLA 1
KEVIN BERRY

A million dollars of goods are stolen... but the insurance company doesn't want to pay out.

Private investigator Danny Ashford is hired to investigate. He and sassy investigative reporter Deepa Banwait soon learn the warehouse break-in was no ordinary robbery.

As they search for the stolen goods, Danny and Deepa discover a wider conspiracy is in play. Robbery escalates to murder. But as they close in on solving the case, they bring themselves closer to a dangerous criminal...

THE POSSUM FUR PLOT is a gripping crime noir mystery that will keep you hooked right up to the dramatic conclusion.
Coming to Amazon in August 2020.

The Quake City Investigations series

About the Author

I'm an Amazon best-selling author living in earthquake-hit Christchurch, New Zealand, where my contemporary novels are set. I'm a night owl and prefer writing late into the night whenever possible.

You can connect with me on:

- http://kevinberrybooks.com
- https://books2read.com/ap/8prEjA/Kevin-Berry
- https://www.amazon.com/Kevin-Berry/e/B00G23NDFI
- https://www.bookbub.com/authors/kevin-berry

Subscribe to my newsletter:

- https://landing.mailerlite.com/webforms/landing/f5k0c7

Also by Kevin Berry

My books span a variety of genres and character voices. Every book I write includes humour because I think reading should be entertaining.

These include:

Contemporary Crime Noir
   The Quake City Investigations series:
   The Drowned Dockworker (prequel novelette)
   Shooting Messengers
   The Possum Fur Plot (coming August 2020)

Humorous Literary Fiction
   Stim
   Kaleidoscope

Interactive Fiction (ages 10-14)
   Stranded Starship
   Duel at Dawn
   Movie Mystery Madness
   Past Present Future
   Secret Project

Dystopian Cyberpunk Science Fiction
   Teleport

My work has so far produced:
   Winner: Sir Julius Vogel Award for Best New Talent (shared);
   Finalist: Sir Julius Vogel Award (5 times, various categories);
   Semifinalist: Kindle Book Review Awards (Literary Fiction, twice);
   Awesome Indies Seal of Approval (twice);

Category Finalist: Eric Hoffer Award;

Amazon (CA) #1 Bestseller ranking in Noir Mysteries and Thrillers;

Amazon (CA) #1 Bestseller ranking in Hard-boiled Mysteries.